Translation
of
Ancient
Poetry

本书为上海外国语大学贤达经济人文学院硕士学位提早培育项目成果

古诗英译教程
——以王维诗歌为例

主　编　冯奇

副主编　张欢　庄甘林　陈启君

WUHAN UNIVERSITY PRESS
武汉大学出版社

图书在版编目(CIP)数据

古诗英译教程:以王维诗歌为例/冯奇主编;张欢,庄甘林,陈启君副主编.—武汉:武汉大学出版社,2023.1
ISBN 978-7-307-23540-3

Ⅰ.古… Ⅱ.①冯… ②张… ③庄… ④陈… Ⅲ.唐诗—英语—翻译—教材 Ⅳ.①I207.22 ②H315.9

中国版本图书馆 CIP 数据核字(2022)第 257737 号

责任编辑:罗晓华   责任校对:汪欣怡   版式设计:马 佳

出版发行:**武汉大学出版社** (430072 武昌 珞珈山)
(电子邮箱:cbs22@ whu.edu.cn 网址:www.wdp.com.cn)
印刷:武汉图物印刷有限公司
开本:787×1092 1/16 印张:11.75 字数:242 千字   插页:1
版次:2023 年 1 月第 1 版   2023 年 1 月第 1 次印刷
ISBN 978-7-307-23540-3   定价:36.00 元

前　　言

　　古诗承载着中华千年文化的精髓，也是古人与当代人对话的一座桥梁。唐代诗人王维是我国山水田园诗派的重要代表人，其诗作继承和发展了谢灵运和陶渊明诗的平淡醇美，在中国诗歌发展史上占有重要地位。王维用约400首古诗记录了其边塞报国的雄心壮志、唐朝的民生百态、战乱后对归隐的向往和对友谊的歌颂。

　　本书从王维诗集中精选54首佳作，其中就包括广为传颂的《使至塞上》，并按照古诗的内容、情感将54首古诗分成6个部分，即边塞、田园、赠答、山水、咏物和送别诗。每个部分的9首古诗进一步按照内容差异，被系统和均匀地分为3章，有助于帮助读者在赏析古诗和学习翻译技巧的同时，掌握中华诗歌分类的体系，从更高的视角去赏析这个文学领域。

　　本书成功地将翻译家赵彦春的王维诗歌英译文转化成了文化翻译教材。本教材通过诗歌主题、内容、情感，对英译文做了系统的分类，使本书内容系统化，利于英语课堂教学的系统展开和知识结构化。此外，本教材设置了译文赏析部分，引导读者领略译文的诗性、文化性、唯美生动的视觉信息、丰富多样的翻译技巧，尤其是在对译文的音韵、字数、词性、句法、语义、译法选择和表达效果上，是广大翻译学习者很好的训练素材。

　　本书每首古诗的译文篇幅精练，解析详尽易懂，适合国内英语专业本科、硕士和中华文化爱好者学习和参考使用。本书的王维古诗英译能够让英语学习者提高中华文化的外译和传播能力，在提升英语翻译功底的同时，提升对中华文化内涵的理解。

　　王维古诗英译不仅仅是一种语言的转换，还要求我们掌握中英诗性的特点、文化百科和历史故事。希望在阅读完本书后，广大外语学习者和爱好者能够受益匪浅，共同传承和传播中华优秀的传统文化。

冯　奇

2022 年 8 月 3 日

目　　录

第三部分　赠答诗

第四部分　山水诗

第五部分 咏物诗

第六部分　送别诗

第一部分 边塞诗

第一章 出征行军

1.1 从 军 行

1.1.1 诗歌背景

王维早年热衷政治，在谪济州司仓参军以后，目睹了出征将士艰苦的军旅生活和发生在边陲的一次战斗，并歌颂了将士们杀敌立功的豪情壮志。这首诗描述了青年士子跨马离家至凯旋的过程。诗的前四句写渡河出军，以备战和应战的各种声响，来成功烘托战争的紧张和激烈的气氛；后四句写战争的经过和战士的胜利，激情大振。诗人以简洁连贯的动词，如"吹角、喧喧、嘶乱、争渡、战声、归来"等，来引发读者对从军应战无限的遐想，善于捕捉特写，语言铿锵有力，体现了诗人高超的语言技巧。全诗充斥着豪放的英雄气概和奋发向上的爱国情绪，具有盛唐边塞诗的激情满怀。

1.1.2 古诗原文

从军行

吹角动行人，

喧喧行人起。

笳悲马嘶乱，

争渡黄河水。

日暮沙漠陲，

战声烟尘里。

尽系名王颈，

归来报天子。

1.1.3　古诗译文

A Border War

A conk toot starts soldiers asleep；

Quick，quick，off bed they rise to leap.

The flute tune sad，the horses cry；

Across the River rush they vie.

The eve sunlight does the sand shroud；

Drowned in the dust is their shouts loud.

Go and get the head of the foe；

To report to Lord we can go.

（赵彦春　译）

◎ 注释

1. the flute：Hu Jia—a reed instrument，an instrument of a northern tribe in ancient China, similar to flute. 笳

2. the River：the Yellow River，the second longest river in China，flowing across Loess Plateau，hence yellow. It is 5,464 kilometers long，with a drainage area of 752,443 square kilometers，having nurtured the Chinese nation，regarded as the cradle of Chinese civilization. 黄河

3. vie：to compete strongly with sb. in order to obtain sth. It refers to the soldiers' competition to cross the Yellow River. 争渡

4. Lord：it refers to the emperor Xuanzong of the Tang Dynasty in the context of this poem. 天子

1.1.4　译文赏析

1. 吹角动行人，喧喧行人起。

译文：A conk toot starts soldiers asleep；

Quick, quick, off bed they rise to leap.

赏析：原文中此分句组采用了重复的手法，重复了"行人"和"喧"字，描绘了士兵在嘈杂人声中纷纷起床的场景，而译者也采用重复的手法，通过重复 quick 来体现士兵起床的催促感；虽然原文未有尾韵，但译文增添了尾韵的修辞，让译文更有诗的特点，如 asleep 和 leap，译文的 leap 不仅翻译了"起"，而且凸显了士兵起床集结的迅速。

2. 笳悲马嘶乱，争渡黄河水。

译文：The flute tune sad, the horses cry;

Across the River rush they vie.

赏析：原文虽无押韵修辞，但译文却增加了尾韵的特点，翻译了诗的风格，而风格的表现方式是多样的，原文采用对偶，译文采用尾韵。"笳"指双方将相遇时，敌军吹起的胡笳（中国北方民族乐器，形如笛子），而译者采用上义词 flute，省略了民族特点，但使外国读者更容易理解。cry 描绘的是马因胡笳声起而引发的嘶叫声，体现马的兴奋。译文中的 vie 指激烈争夺，不仅和前句押韵，还巧妙地还原了"争"所体现的双方争先渡河的场面。

3. 日暮沙漠陲，战声烟尘里。

译文：The eve sunlight does the sand shroud;

Drowned in the dust is their shouts loud.

赏析：同上一句组一样，译文比原文多出了句组内尾韵的特征，如 shroud 和 loud。译文的另一特征是两句长度非常接近对偶的程度。前句的"日暮"和"沙漠陲"描绘了战斗一直持续到太阳落到沙丘边缘的时候，而译文的 eve sunlight 和 the sand shroud 描绘的是沙漠覆盖傍晚阳光的意象。译文的 shouts loud 描绘了那烟尘弥漫的战场上传来的厮杀声，烘托了战争的激烈。

4. 尽系名王颈，归来报天子。

译文：Go and get the head of the foe;

To report to Lord we can go.

赏析：原文与上一句组形成尾韵，如"子"和"里"，而译者选择在句组内押尾韵，如 foe 与 go。原文可理解为战士们歼灭敌军，用绳子套在敌酋颈上，带回来献给天子。然而，译者将原文译成了祈使句，以动词原形开头，更像指挥官在战场上对士兵的命令和号召，其时态更集中于战斗中的目的，而原文时态更集中于战斗后的成果。因原文字面无时态信息，其时态有多种可能，所以译文可以灵活地解读原文的时态。

1.2 陇西行

1.2.1 诗歌背景

陇西指陇山以西的地域，在今甘肃省陇西县以东。《陇西行》是王维借用乐府的旧题在盛唐时期(公元737年)创作的五言诗。全诗整体呈现了匈奴围城和边防告急的形势，并从军使送书的片段来侧面烘托战争将至的局势。全文没有正面描绘激烈战斗的过程，而是通过军使送书的紧急和迷茫壮阔的关山飞雪图景来烘托边关紧张的局势。在写到烽火台因不明原因而断烟时，全诗戛然而止，不仅干脆利落，也给读者留下了遐想空间。

1.2.2 古诗原文

陇 西 行

十里一走马，
五里一扬鞭。
都护军书至，
匈奴围酒泉。
关山正飞雪，
烽戍断无烟。

1.2.3 古诗译文

A Frontier Poem

Four miles the horse does run in haste,

Two miles finished at one whip raised.

The governor's order comes then:

Wine Spring's besieged by the Hun men.

Snow flies over pass and mountain,

No more smoke from any beacon.

（赵彦春 译）

◎ 注释

1. A Frontier Poem：the name of an ancient Chinese poem，which belongs to the folk songs of Yue Fu. 陇西行

2. governor：it refers to the governor of Du Hu Department in this poem，which is one of the six military organs established to govern the western regions of China in the Tang Dynasty. 都护

3. Wine Spring：a city called Chiuch'uan if transliterated，in today's Kansu Province. 酒泉

4. Hun men：Hun invaders from north and west of China. Huns have been regarded as barbarians in Chinese history although they are of the same origin as Chinese，originating from Old Ch'iang. 匈奴

5. beacon：it refers to the ancient sentry of frontier defense，which sends the warning of coming enemy by fire and smoke. 烽戍

1.2.4 译文赏析

1. 十里一走马，五里一扬鞭。

译文：Four miles the horse does run in haste，

Two miles finished at one whip raised.

赏析：译文和原文都用了词语重复策略，如"里"和 miles，以象征动作的重复性。原文与下一句组形成尾韵，如"鞭"和"泉"，而译文则选择在句组内押尾韵，如 haste 和 raised。原文"十里"和"五里"在译文中被转化成了英文单位 mile，并分别被换算成了 four miles 和 two miles(1 英里＝3. 218688 里)，增强了译文的可理解性。

2. 都护军书至，匈奴围酒泉。

译文：The governor's order comes then：

Wine Spring's besieged by the Hun men.

赏析：原文该句与上下组的句尾形成尾韵，如"鞭""泉""烟"，而译者采用组内分句尾韵来翻译原文的押韵修辞手法，如 then 和 men。然而，原文的尾韵词在译文中未用于尾韵，可见译者翻译的对象是尾韵的修辞手法，而非尾韵所采用的词。

3. 关山正飞雪，烽戍断无烟。

译文：Snow flies over pass and mountain,

No more smoke from any beacon.

赏析：译文采用句组内尾韵的手法，如 mountain 和 beacon，来对应原文与上一组句形成的尾韵。译文和原文共同描写了边关山岳大雪纷飞，烽火联系不知何因而中断的情形，留给读者对后续情形的遐想空间。

1.3 燕支行

1.3.1 诗歌背景

《燕支行》是王维 21 岁时写的一首以军旅边塞生活为题材的七言歌行体诗，这类诗是一类可以配乐歌唱的诗歌体裁。全诗共 24 句，可分为 3 个段落。第一段有 4 句，记叙了将军出征，皇帝亲自为他推车，数千位大臣为他设宴送行，以壮丽的宫殿和庄严肃穆的五陵来衬托将军的英雄气概。第二段的 8 句引用了历史上著名的英雄将领来形容这位将军，表达了他不愿在京城过安逸生活，而要去抵御外敌、镇守边关的决心，也为下段征战沙场做好铺垫。第三段为全诗高潮，诗人用夸张的手法、急促的节奏和生动的描绘，来记叙这位将军艰难的行军、英勇的作战和辉煌的战果，热烈地歌颂了将军的雄才大略。

1.3.2 古诗原文

燕 支 行

汉家天将才且雄，

来时谒帝明光宫。

万乘亲推双阙下，

千官出饯五陵东。

誓辞甲第金门里，

身作长城玉塞中。

卫霍才堪一骑将，

朝廷不数贰师功。

赵魏燕韩多劲卒，

关西侠少何咆勃。

报仇只是闻尝胆。

饮酒不曾妨刮骨。

画戟雕戈白日寒，

连旗大旆黄尘没。

叠鼓遥翻瀚海波，

鸣笳乱动天山月。

麒麟锦带佩吴钩，

飒沓青骊跃紫骝。

拔剑已断天骄臂，

归鞍共饮月支头。

汉兵大呼一当百，

虏骑相看哭且愁。

教战虽令赴汤火，

终知上将先伐谋。

1.3.3　古诗译文

Marching to Mt. Rouge

The Han general with great talent and flair

Calls on His Majesty at Palace Glare.

Most High pushes his cart out Phoenix Gate;

East of Five Tombs courtiers for farewell wait.

He makes an oath and leaves his golden hall；

At the fortress he will be a great wall.

He'll outdo Watch and Huo，commanders best

And General Li，who did foes and steeds arrest.

He's many gallants from Chao，Yan，Han and Way，

And those strongmen from West，who boldly sway.

He'd taste bitter bile to revenge the land

And drink while bone-scraping pain he could stand.

Halberds and spears wave，and the sun looks cold；

The sand kicked off will drown the flags，behold.

The war drum beaten hard the desert shakes；

The Hun flute sadly played the pass moon quakes.

The unicorn belt and Wu hook both shine

Black steeds gallop，brown horses neigh，all fine.

Swiftly sword swayed，a Hun arm is chopped off；

Drinking out of skulls，at Jouchih they scoff.

Han soldiers fight o'erwhelmingly and shout；

Hun dragoons cry wretchedly，what a rout.

When ordered to attack，fighters will burst，

But a good general should plot the fight first.

（赵彦春　译）

◎ 注释

1. Mt. Rouge：the Rouge Mountains，a range of mountains in today's Ope-arms（Changyeh），
   Kansu Province，lush with pines and cypresses and various kinds of plants and grass，and
   inhabited by Huns in the Han Dynasty. 燕支

2. Palace Glare：a Han palace built in the fourth year of Emperor Martial's reign，that is 101
   B.C. 明光宫

3. Phoenix Gate：the gate of the imperial palace with five phoenix towers on it. 双阙

4. Five Tombs：five mausoleums of five Han emperor on the north bank of the Wei. 五陵

5. Watch and Huo: referring to two famous generals in the Han Dynasty, Blue Watch (? -106 B. C.), Ch'ing Wei if transliterated, and Swift Huo (140 B. C. -117 B. C.). Both generals were the first-ranking generals in the Han Dynasty. 卫霍

6. General Li: Broad Li (? -119 B. C.) in full name, Kuang Li if transliterated, a renowned general who won many battles against the Huns in the Han Dynasty. 贰师

7. Chao: the State of Chao (403 B. C. -222 B. C.), a vassal state in the Spring and Autumn Period, one of the Seven Powers in the Warring States Period. 赵

8. Yan: the State of Yan (1, 044 B. C. -222 B. C.), a vassal state in the Spring and Autumn Period, one of the Seven Powers in the Warring States Period. 燕

9. Han: the State of Han (403. B. C. -230 B. C.) a vassal state in the Spring and Autumn Period, one of the Seven Powers in the Warring States Period. 韩

10. Way: the State of Way (403 B. C. -225 B. C.), a vassal state of Chough, one of the Seven Powers in the Warring States Period. 魏

11. West: alias Western Regions, the areas inhabited by Huns and other nomadic people governed by China, for example, the Han Empire and the T'ang Empire, generally stretching from Jade Gate Pass and Sun Pass to Pamir Plateau and Balkhash Lake, and sometimes even to Caspian Sea and Black Sea. 关西

12. Hun: one of barbaric nomadic Asian people who frequently invaded China, a general term referring to all northern or western invaders. 天骄, 虏骑

13. Jouchih: indicating an area around Hohsi Corridor and the ethnic group or language bearing the name. 月支

1.3.4　译文赏析

1. 汉家天将才且雄，来时谒帝明光宫。
   万乘亲推双阙下，千官出饯五陵东。

译文: The Han general with great talent and flair; Calls on His Majesty at Palace Glare. Most High pushes his cart out Phoenix Gate; East of Five Tombs courtiers for farewell wait.

赏析: 原文在两句组间押尾韵，而译者选择在各句组内押尾韵，利于还原尾韵的修辞，也减少了译文押韵的难度。"才且雄"表达了将军的雄才大略，译文以 talent 和 flair

(天资)的语义重复来强调将军的才能,与原文表现手法一致。"双阙"为凤凰图布局的皇宫建筑群,其中"阙"为凤凰,因此被译成 Phoenix Gate,指地名。

2. 麒麟锦带佩吴钩,飒沓青骊跃紫骝。

译文:The unicorn belt and Wu hook both shine;

Black steeds gallop, brown horses neigh, all fine.

赏析:原文在句组内押韵,译文在同样的位置还原了尾韵修辞。原文描写了将军身着华丽战袍,手持锐利兵器,一马当先地向敌人冲去。"麒麟"为中国神兽,直译会使外国读者不理解,所以译者选用外国神兽 unicorn,来形成文化符号的对等。

3. 拔剑已断天骄臂,归鞍共饮月支头。

　　汉兵大呼一当百,虏骑相看哭且愁。

译文:Swiftly sword swayed, a Hun arm is chopped off; Drinking out of skulls, at Jouchih they scoff.

Han soldiers fight o'erwhelmingly and shout; Hun dragoons cry wretchedly, what a rout.

赏析:原文在句组间押尾韵,而译者选择在句组内押尾韵,并在第二句组内同时押头韵和尾韵。"一当百"以数量来凸显汉军势不可挡的攻势,被译成副词 o'erwhelmingly(压倒性地),和原文画面一致。"虏骑"指敌方骑兵,其译文 dragoons 能体现敌方的凶悍,也与 cry wretchedly 和 rout 形成鲜明的对比。

第二章　剑拔弩张

2.1　使至塞上

2.1.1　诗歌背景

唐玄宗开元二十四年(公元736年)，吐蕃发兵攻打唐属国小勃律(今克什米尔的吉尔吉特)。公元737年春，河西节度副大使崔希逸在青涤西大破吐蕃军。为了将王维排挤出朝廷，唐玄宗命王维以监察御史的身份奉使凉州，出塞宣慰，察访军情，并任河西节度使判官。这首诗即作于此次出塞途中。《使至塞上》描绘了塞外奇特壮丽的风光，表现了诗人对不畏艰苦、以身许国的守边战士的爱国精神的赞美；此诗叙事精练简洁，画面奇丽壮美。

2.1.2　古诗原文

使至塞上

单车欲问边，

属国过居延。

征蓬出汉塞，

归雁入胡天。

大漠孤烟直，

长河落日圆。

萧关逢候骑，

都护在燕然。

2.1.3 古诗译文

To the Front as an Envoy

To inspect the front I drive down;

Now thru the vassal's Chuyan Town.

Thistledown past Han Fortress flies;

Wild geese fleet into the Huns' skies.

O'er the wild smoke lonely curls straight;

To the river the sun round sets late.

At Hsiao Pass I meet a scout; the man

Tells me the general's at Yanjan.

（赵彦春 译）

◎ 注释

1. Chuyan Town：also known as Chuyan Sea, in today's Inner Mongolia, 80 kilometers from Ope-arms, that is, today's Changyeh, Kansu Province. 居延

2. thistledown：an important image in Chinese literature, a metaphor for vagrants or strayers. 征蓬

3. Han Fortress：a general term referring to any border pass of Han. 汉塞

4. Hun：one of barbaric nomadic Asian people who frequently invaded China, a general term referring to all northern or western invaders and aliens. 胡

5. Hsiao Pass：name of an old pass, southeast of today's Firm Plain (Kuyuan), Ninghsia Hui's Autonomous Region. 萧关

6. Yanjan：Mt. Yanjan, a mountain located in present-day Mongolia. It is usually used to imply an enemy with military threat. 燕然

2.1.4 译文赏析

1. 单车欲问边，属国过居延。

译文：To inspect the front I drive down；

　　　　Now thru the vassal's Chuyan Town.

赏析：译文和原文都采用尾韵的修辞手法；译文的两个分句在字数上基本一致，都有四个实词；译文和原文意思对等，都表达了作者去边塞的目的和途经的城市；译者灵活地转换了动词和介词的词性，如"欲"译成 to，"过"译成 thru。

2. 征蓬出汉塞，归雁入胡天。

译文：Thistledown past Han Fortress flies；

　　　　Wild geese fleet into the Huns' skies.

赏析：原文两分句中间押韵，如"出"和"入"，与译文 past 和 fleet 形成押韵对等；原文与上一组句子押尾韵，如"延"和"天"，而译文的尾韵处理为组内尾韵，如 flies 和 skies；"征蓬"指枯干的蓬草，比喻王维像随风而去的蓬草一样，出临汉塞，而译文的 Thistledown 为蓟花的冠毛，也有随风而起的属性，与原文意象对等。

3. 大漠孤烟直，长河落日圆。

译文：O'er the wild smoke lonely curls straight；

　　　　To the river the sun round sets late.

赏析：原文分句组末尾与上组末尾押韵，如"圆"和"天"，而译文则采用组内分句末尾押韵的手法，如 straight 和 late；译文两分句实词的字数对等；译者将"大漠"译成 wild，并以语气词 o'er 烘托出沙漠的广阔；为求押尾韵，译者采用增译法，添加了 late，描绘了渐进性日落的意象。

4. 萧关逢候骑，都护在燕然。

译文：At Hsiao Pass I meet a scout；the man

　　　　Tells me the general's at Yanjan.

赏析：原文的"然"与上一分句组末尾的"圆"一起形成尾韵，而译文选择分句组内押尾韵，如 man 和 Yanjan；因前分句难以找到尾韵词，译者将后分句的 the man 并入前分句；译文采用了一般现在时，在于引领读者身临其境，体验诗人当时的感受；译者采用了增译法，增加了诗人所见但原文未写的部分，如 the man tells me。

2.2　出　塞　作

2.2.1　诗歌背景

《出塞作》为王维在边塞任御史监察时所作。全诗上半部分通过胡人打猎的浩大声势，烘托出边塞剑拔弩张的紧张局势。第 3、4 句描写了边塞唐军健将骑马时的勇猛强悍和射雕时沉着应战的心态。全诗的下半部分则凸显了唐军斗志昂扬的士气和势如破竹的进军速度，并以唐军的胜利和论功行赏收尾。诗歌的前半部分通过对比胡人的咄咄逼人与唐军的沉着冷静，衬托出了唐军的作战有方和攻防兼备，以冷静压倒对方的凌人气势。后半部分描写了唐军的胜利和对功臣的嘉奖，体现了诗人对唐军胜利的赞颂和对盛唐国力强盛的自豪感。

2.2.2　古诗原文

出　塞　作

居延城外猎天骄，
白草连天野火烧。
暮云空碛时驱马，
秋日平原好射雕。
护羌校尉朝乘障，
破虏将军夜渡辽。
玉靶角弓珠勒马，
汉家将赐霍嫖姚。

2.2.3　古诗译文

Beyond the Border

Out of Chuyan, the Huns are hunting game;

Dried grass rolling to the sky is aflame.

On dust-lit sand I give my horse free rein；

It's time to shoot hawks on the autumn plain.

Ch'iang Governor climbs up the barring height；

Beat Foe General crosses the Liao at night.

Inlaid sword， horned bow and pearled steed；behold

Will be granted to those like Swift so bold.

（赵彦春　译）

◎ 注释

1. Chuyan：also known as Chuyan Sea, in today's Inner Mongolia, 80 kilometers from Ope-arms, that is, today's Changyeh, Kansu Province. 居延

2. Hun：one of barbaric nomadic Asian people who frequently invaded China, a general term referring to all northern or western invaders and aliens. 胡

3. Ch'iang：an ethnic group living in the west of China, having the same origin as Chinese. 羌

4. Beat Foe General：title of a military commander in ancient China. 破虏将军

5. Liao：the Liao River, mainly in today's Liaoning Province. 辽

6. Swift：Swift Huo （140 B. C. -117 B. C. ）, P'iaoyao Huo if transliterated, a renowned general, prominent strategist and patriotic hero in the Han Dynasty. He made his first show at 17, leading 800 fierce cavalrymen to penetrate the enemy lines and defeat the Huns. Swift fought against the Huns in three major wars and each time returned with victory. He died of a disease at 23, leaving his achievements as the highest glory for Chinese military commanders. 霍嫖姚

2.2.4　译文赏析

1. 居延城外猎天骄，白草连天野火烧。

译文：Out of Chuyan, the Huns are hunting game；
Dried grass rolling to the sky is aflame.

赏析：译文和原文都采用了尾韵手法，如 game 和 aflame 对"骄"和"烧"；原文前分句无主语，而译者采用增译法将"猎天骄"的主语在译文中还原，即胡人（Huns）；后分句中

17

的"野火"与动词"烧"在意象上重复，因此译者采用减译法在译文中将"野火"省略；此分句组描写了胡人在城外狩猎和野外随风飘扬的枯草在火中燃烧的情景，烘托了边塞战争局势的紧张。

2. **暮云空碛时驱马，秋日平原好射雕**。

译文：On dust-lit sand I give my horse free rein;

It's time to shoot hawks on the autumn plain.

赏析：原文第 4 句的"雕"与第 2 句的"烧"形成尾韵，而译者则在第 3、4 句间形成尾韵，如 rein 和 plain；第 4 句的 plain 与第 2 句的 aflame 也在尾韵上非常接近；为形成尾韵，译者将位于句中的"平原"译在了句子的末尾，体现了译者找音近词、调整排序、形成尾韵的思路；原文的地点状语"暮云空碛"和"秋日平原"位于句首，而译文中的"秋日平原"则位于句末，体现了句型随押韵的需要而灵活调整的翻译权重。

3. **护羌校尉朝乘障，破虏将军夜渡辽**。

译文：Ch'iang Governor climbs up the barring height;

Beat Foe General crosses the Liao at night.

赏析：原文分句组的"辽"与上一句组末尾的"雕"形成尾韵；译者则选择在分句组内形成尾韵，如 height 和 night；"护羌校尉"源于汉代拿着符节保护西羌的武官，这里指唐朝在居廷守边的将领，所以译为 Ch'iang Governor；"朝乘障"指早晨登上遮虏障，而遮虏障指西汉时为了防止匈奴内侵，在居延一带修筑的一种防御工事，所以译为 the barring height，指铁条或木条做成的路障；"破虏将军"指汉昭帝时中郎将范明友，他带领兵马渡过辽河，平定了辽东乌桓的叛乱，在此诗中指唐军将领，而译文 Beat Foe General 保留了中文字义特点。

4. **玉靶角弓珠勒马，汉家将赐霍嫖姚**。

译文：Inlaid sword, horned bow and pearled steed, behold

Will be granted to those like Swift so bold.

赏析：原文分句组与上一句组形成尾韵，如"姚"与"辽"同为元音/ao/，而译者选择在句组内押尾韵，如 behold 和 bold；"玉靶"和"角弓"分别指以玉为柄的宝剑和兽角装饰的弓，分别被译为 inlaid sword(镶嵌的剑)和 horned bow(兽角弓)，但"玉"字因字数限制而被减译；"珠勒马"指用珠宝装饰的马勒口，而译文 pearled steed(镶嵌珠宝的壮马)完整地还原了该意象；"霍嫖姚"指西汉抗击匈奴的嫖姚校尉霍去病，在此诗中借指在青海战败吐蕃的崔希逸，而译文 Swift (迅速敏捷) 是 Swift Huo 的简写，对应"嫖姚"的矫捷强劲。此句组的译文描写了唐军功臣论功行赏的画面，体现了唐朝国力的强盛。

2.3　少年行四首

2.3.1　诗歌背景

《少年行四首》是王维早年所作的七言组诗，歌颂了长安少年游侠的豪情壮志。四首诗分别描述了少年游侠的豪饮酣醉、精忠报国的壮志、骁勇善战的气概和有功无赏的遭遇。第一首诗借用美酒、骏马、高楼、垂柳的意象，来衬托少年游侠的意气风发。第二首诗描写了游侠出征边塞，借汉事喻唐，用羽林郎和骠骑来衬托少年游侠的才能。第三首描写了少年的骁勇善战，以"一身"对战"虏骑千重"来将少年塑造成孤胆英雄的形象。第四首诗写少年游侠有功无赏，在君臣欢宴、云台论功时，领赏者却变成了将军，而浴血奋战的勇士反遭冷落。这种欲抑先扬的手法，有力地体现了不平之声。该组诗押韵的特点突出，许多诗句同时兼有头韵和尾韵。

2.3.2　古诗原文

少年行四首

其一
新丰美酒斗十千，
咸阳游侠多少年。
相逢意气为君饮，
系马高楼垂柳边。

其二
出身仕汉羽林郎，
初随骠骑战渔阳。

孰知不向边庭苦，

纵死犹闻侠骨香。

其三

一身能擘两雕弧，

虏骑千重只似无。

偏坐金鞍调白羽，

纷纷射杀五单于。

其四

汉家君臣欢宴终，

高议云台论战功。

天子临轩赐侯印，

将军佩出明光宫。

2.3.3 古诗译文

The Lads，Four Poems

No. 1

The Newrich wine is as precious as gold；

The Allshine lads all have a resolve bold.

They take a long swallow to show their pride，

Their horses tied to the willows inn-side.

No. 2

He leaves home to be an Armed Escort guard；

And follows Swift to Fishshine and fights hard.

The frontier life is hard，everyone knows；

E'en if he dies，he'll smell of a sweet rose.

No. 3

With two hands he draws a carved bow with might

The swarming horsemen are nothing at all

Astride his steed, he adjusts the plume white

And all those Hun chieftains are shot to fall.

No. 4

Lord and peers celebrate their feat of war；

On Cloud Mound they judge who's done less or more.

His Majesty confers Seal of Marquis；

The general's prize shines out of the palace.

（赵彦春　译）

◎ 注释

1. the Newrich wine：the best and most expensive wine in the Tang Dynasty. Newrich was an old town of Han, in today's Lintung County, Sha'nhsi Province, well-known for its good wine. The town was built by Pang Liu in imitation of his hometown Rich County, i. e., today's Rich County, Chiangsu Province. 新丰美酒

2. the Allshine lads：boys in Allshine. Allshine, Hsienyang if transliterated, was the capital of the Ch'in Empire. It is so called because all its rivers and mountains can get sunshine from all around. 咸阳少年

3. Armed Escort：imperial guarding Corps, established by Emperor Martial in Western Han. 羽林郎

4. Swift：Swift Huo（140 B. C. -117 B. C.）, P'iaoyao Huo if transliterated, a renowned general, prominent strategist and patriotic hero in the Han Dynasty. He made his first show at 17, leading 800 fierce cavalrymen to penetrate the enemy lines and defeat the Huns. Swift fought against the Huns in three major wars and each time returned with victory. He died of a disease at 23, leaving his achievements as the highest glory for Chinese military commanders. 骠骑

5. Fishshine：Fishshine Prefecture, today's Chi District, Tientsin. 渔阳

6. Hun chieftains：leaders of the Hun troops. 单于

7. Cloud Mound：a peak of Mt. Flora，which is one of the Five Mountains in China，representing the west. 云台

8. Seal of Marquis：a gold seal with a purple ribbon，representing the power or status of a marquis. 侯印

2.3.4　译文赏析

1. 新丰美酒斗十千，咸阳游侠多少年。
    相逢意气为君饮，系马高楼垂柳边。

译文：The Newrich wine is as precious as gold；The Allshine lads all have a resolve bold. They take a long swallow to show their pride；Their horses tied to the willows inn-side.

赏析：原文同时在四句的头、尾押韵，头押/xi/韵，尾押/n/韵。译文能做到与原文的头尾韵同步，四句头押/ð/韵，两句组尾分别押/əuld/和/aɪd/。"新丰"指古县城名，为今日的陕西省临潼（tóng）县东北，古时盛产名贵的美酒。译者在处理该地名时，没有简单地采用拼音，而是跳过原文的音，去翻译原文的词义，即新（new）丰（rich），以增强译文的可理解性。"咸阳"为秦朝都城，此处代指长安，位于陕西省八百里秦川腹地，渭水穿南，山水俱阳，故称咸阳。为突出山水俱阳的特性，咸阳被译成 Allshine，意为万物俱阳。

2. 出身仕汉羽林郎，初随骠骑战渔阳。
    孰知不向边庭苦，纵死犹闻侠骨香。

译文：He leaves home to be an Armed Escort guard；And follows Swift to Fishshine and fights hard.

The frontier life is hard，everyone knows；E'en if he dies，he'll smell of a sweet rose.

赏析：原文四句共有三处头韵，即"出""初""孰"，三处尾韵，即"郎""阳""香"。译者选择在两句组内押尾韵，以对等原文尾韵特征，如 guard 和 hard、knows 和 rose，但其头韵特征未能译出。"羽林郎"为汉代禁卫军官名，用于象征少年的才能，被译成 Armed Escort guard，译出了该职位的功能和形象。"骠骑"指骠骑大将军霍去病，Swift 象征雨燕穿梭敏捷，而"骠"指黄骠马，喻义骁勇飞骑，与 Swift 物种不同，但特征一致。"渔阳"为汉朝常与匈奴交战处，Fishshine 译出了地名的字面意义和具体形象。

3. 一身能擘两雕弧，虏骑千重只似无。
   偏坐金鞍调白羽，纷纷射杀五单于。

译文：With two hands he draws a carved bow with might; The swarming horsemen are nothing at all

Astride his steed, he adjusts the plume white; And all those Hun chieftains are shot to fall.

赏析：原文在两句组内押尾韵，如"弧"和"无"、"羽"和"于"，而译文则选择在两句组间形成尾韵，如 might 和 white、all 和 fall。"虏骑千重"指敌方大军压境的包围之势，与"一身"的孤胆英雄形成对比。译文未出现这种数量的对比，而是将数量表现的敌军势头译成了 swarming。"一身"被译成了 With two hands，也体现了译者注重古诗画面的再现，而非字面的对等。

4. 汉家君臣欢宴终，高议云台论战功。
   天子临轩赐侯印，将军佩出明光宫。

译文：Lord and peers celebrate their feat of war; On Cloud Mound they judge who's done less or more.

His Majesty confers Seal of Marquis; The general's prize shines out of the palace.

赏析：原文三句末尾同押尾韵，即"终""功""宫"，而译文在两句组内押尾韵，如 war 和 more、Marquis 和 palace，其修辞手法对等，但修辞位置不同。"云台"指东汉洛阳宫中的座台，二十八个开国功臣的像曾被明帝下令画在台上，史称"云台二十八将"，Cloud Mound 译出了"云台"的字义。最后两句写了天子在殿栏前赐予列侯印，将军佩着印绶走出明光宫。"侯印"指官印，被译成 Seal of Marquis，其中 Marquis 为欧洲的侯爵，位列伯爵和公爵之间，与中国的"列侯"官位对等。

第三章　功高无赏

3.1　陇头吟

3.1.1　诗歌背景

　　《陇头吟》是王维借用乐府旧题写的边塞诗。陇头指陇山一带，大致在今陕西陇县到甘肃清水县一带。全诗用"长安少年""陇上行人""关西老将""苏武"四类人物，以及戍楼看星、月夜吹笛、驻马流泪的生活情景，烘托出了边塞生活寂寞悲凉的意境。全诗反映了边塞艰苦的生活和老将功高无赏的悲愤，具有广泛的社会意义。

3.1.2　古诗原文

陇　头　吟

长安少年游侠客，
夜上戍楼看太白。
陇头明月迥临关，
陇上行人夜吹笛。
关西老将不胜愁，
驻马听之双泪流。
身经大小百馀战，

麾下偏裨万户侯。

苏武才为典属国，

节旄落尽海西头。

3.1.3　古诗译文

A Song at Mt. Ridge

A Long Peace lad would be a gallant knight;

On a watchtower he asks Venus at night.

The mountain and pass are paled by the moon;

A vagrant paled as well plays a flute tune.

The frontier general old stricken with woe

Stops his horse to listen and his tears flow.

He's fought a hundred small or large battles

And his men have been peered with all titles.

Wu Su was named for mere vassal affairs;

By North Sea worn off were his tally hairs!

（赵彦春　译）

◎ 注释

1. Mt. Ridge：a mountain meandering on the border of Hsa'anhsi and Kansu. 陇头

2. Long Peace：Chang'an if transliterated, the capital of China in the Tang Dynasty, and the provinical capital of today's Sha'anhsi Province. 长安

3. Venus：the second planet closest to the sun, as is called Morning Star in the morning and Evening Star in the evening. Chinese ancients believed that Venus could predict military affairs. 太白

4. Wu Su：Wu Su（140 B. C. -60 B. C.）, a minister of Han. On his diplomatic mission, Su was detained. The Huns tried to make him surrender with threats and promises, only to fail. Then, he was sent to North Sea to be a shepherd. Through all kinds of hardship, Su finally came back to Han after 19 years' detention. During the 19 years, Su Wu had never

surrendered. 苏武

5. North Sea: present-day Lake Baikal, the deepest lake in the world, today's Siberia, Russia. 海西头

3.1.4 译文赏析

1. 长安少年游侠客，夜上戍楼看太白。

译文：A Long Peace lad would be a gallant knight;

On a watchtower he asks Venus at night.

赏析：原文无押韵修辞，其诗歌特征在于对偶，但译文增加了尾韵的特征，来体现译文的诗性，如 knight 和 night。"长安"为唐朝首都地名，译者没有直译其拼音，而是译出地名的深层内涵，Long Peace 舍弃了原文语言形式而再现了内涵。"游侠客"泛指古代豪爽好交游、轻生重义、勇于排难解纷的人，而译文的 knight 原指欧洲中世纪时受过正式军事训练的骑兵和荣誉称号，与中国的"游侠客"在形象和所具备的品质上一致。戍楼(shù lóu)指边防驻军的瞭望塔，译成 watchtower。文中最妙的翻译是"太白"，这个词指太白金星，在文中指客观世界的天体金星，Venus 在西方也指金星，象征美神维纳斯，两者虽然象征的神灵不同，但指向同一天体。

2. 陇头明月迥临关，陇上行人夜吹笛。

译文：The mountain and pass are paled by the moon;

A vagrant paled as well plays a flute tune.

赏析：原文在句头采用词语重复的修辞，强调两句写的是同一地点，而译文对应的修辞是尾韵。陇头，指陇山一带，大致在今陕西陇县到甘肃清水县一带。译文未直接译出地名的中文特性，而是将地点的地形特点译出，即 the mountain and pass。从整体上，可看出译者此处更强调原文和译文所呈现的视觉信息的对等性。

3. 关西老将不胜愁，驻马听之双泪流。

译文：The frontier general old stricken with woe;

Stops his horse to listen and his tears flow.

赏析：原文和译文同押尾韵，"愁"与"流"的押韵强调了悲伤的情绪，译文的 woe(悲叹)和 flow 也起着同样的作用。关西指函谷关或潼关以西的地区，在译文中被模糊处理为

frontier(边关)，体现了译者在精确信息和模糊信息间来回切换的技巧。此句组描写了关西老将停马听笛声，不禁老泪横流的情景。

4. **身经大小百馀战，麾下偏裨万户侯。**

   苏武才为典属国，节旄落尽海西头。

译文：He's fought a hundred small or large battles；

And his men have been peered with all titles.

Wu Su was named for mere vassal affairs；

By North Sea worn off were his tally hairs！

赏析：原文采用句组间尾韵，而译文采用句组内押尾韵。"麾下"和"偏裨"分别指部下和将佐，译文用 he 和 his 代指上句提到的"关西老将"，译出了"身经大小百馀战"中隐形的主语。"典属国"指汉代掌藩属国事务的官职，品位不高，在诗中指苏武出使匈奴被留，牧羊 19 年，回国后也只做了个"典属国"小官。vassal affairs 指属国事物，译出了"典属国"官职的功能。"节旄"指旄节上所缀的牦牛尾饰物，而 tally hairs 特指牦牛尾上的毛发，以比喻苏武 19 年流放的时光飞逝。

3.2　李　陵　咏

3.2.1　诗歌背景

王维创作此诗时，年仅十九岁。《李陵咏》是一首五言"复古"诗，语言质朴流畅，不像六朝诗的词语那样雕琢华丽。比起追求诗歌语言的形式美，此诗更注重传达人的情怀寄托。《李陵咏》记叙的是身为将门虎子的李陵将军，刚成年就具备军事才能和凌云壮志，在沙漠中骁勇善战，长驱直入匈奴人的壁垒之中，但因援军迟迟未到，而被迫投降的故事。诗的末尾借用了苏武牧羊的典故，歌颂了李陵对国家的忠诚，也对其不幸的结局表示同情。

3.2.2　古诗原文

李　陵　咏

汉家李将军，

三代将门子。

结发有奇策,

少年成壮士。

长驱塞上儿,

深入单于垒。

旌旗列相向,

箫鼓悲何已。

日暮沙漠陲,

战声烟尘里。

将令骄虏灭,

岂独名王侍。

既失大军援,

遂婴穷庐耻。

少小蒙汉恩,

何堪坐思此。

深衷欲有报,

投躯未能死。

引领望子卿,

非君谁相理。

3.2.3 古诗译文

Ode to Ridge Li

The Han had a glorious name Li,

Three generals, generations three.

Ridge came of age with a great plan;

Though young, he became a great man.

To the front, ahead he did go,

Go ahead to Chanyu, the foe.

Banners and streamers made a line,

Flutes and war drums did sadly whine.

Dusk fell on the desert so vast；

The war cries stirred up dust，up cast.

The general would all terminate，

Not just the chieftain subjugate.

But in need he received no aid；

To surrender there he was made.

He'd been favored by Han since young；

With such a disgrace he was stung.

His Majesty's grace he'd repay；

He'd die for that to have his day.

He raised his eyes towards Wu Su：

Who can understand me now，who?

（赵彦春 译）

◎ 注释

1. Ridge Li：Ling Li（134 B. C. -74 B. C.），the grandson of the outstanding General Broad Li. Ridge Li surrendered to the Huns after defeat，and completely broke off with the Han court when Lord Martial killed his family，believing the rumor. 李陵

2. Ridge came of age：it refers to the adolescence of Ridge family members. 结发

3. Chanyu：the title of a Hun chieftain. 单于

4. Han：the powerful Han Empire（202 B. C. -220 A. D.）founded by Pang Liu. 汉

5. Wu Su：Wu Su（140 B. C. -60 B. C.），a minister of Han. On his diplomatic mission，Su was detained. The Huns tried to make him surrender with threats and promises，only to fail. Then，he was sent to North Sea，today's Baikal Lake in Siberia，Russia，to be a shepherd. Through all kinds of hardship，Su finally came back to Han after 19 years' detention. During the 19 years，Wu Su had never surrendered. 苏武

3.2.4 译文赏析

1. 汉家李将军，三代将门子。
结发有奇策，少年成壮士。

译文：The Han had a glorious name Li, Three generals, generations three.

Ridge came of age with a great plan; Though young, he became a great man.

赏析：原文的押韵特点是句组内的头韵和句组间的尾韵，而对应的译文则统一在句组内押尾韵。"李将军"指李陵，字少卿，西汉名将李广之孙，译文以 glorious name Li 再现了"李将军"伟大的外延义。译文对"三"字的重复，以及"代"和"将"同词根 gene 的译文，使得译文朗朗上口。"结发"指古代男子自成童开始束发，比喻初成年。其译文 Ridge came of age 特指初成年的李陵，其字面义为到了成年期的李陵，以动词短语翻译了名词"结发"。

2. 长驱塞上儿，深入单于垒。

译文：To the front, ahead he did go, Go ahead to Chanyu, the foe.

赏析：译文比原文多出了尾韵的特征，更具诗性。"塞上儿"在文中指塞上的匈奴人，译文将其模糊为地点 To the front。"单于"是匈奴人对他们部落联盟首领的专称，喻义广大之貌。"单于"本身是异域词汇，无汉字的字面喻义，而译者选择保留其异域性，译出其音，而非泛化成 king 或 chief of tribe。然而，外国读者对其词义的理解，则需要依赖注解或百科全书。

3. 日暮沙漠陲，战声烟尘里。
　　将令骄虏灭，岂独名王侍。

译文：Dusk fell on the desert so vast; The war cries stirred up dust, up cast.

The general would all terminate, Not just the chieftain subjugate.

赏析：原文句组间押尾韵，译文在两句组内押尾韵，比原文更有节奏感。"沙漠陲"指沙漠的边沿，文中用于指战斗持续到了日落沙丘的景象，译文中的 vast 属于增译法，凸显沙漠的广袤，也形成了尾韵。"骄虏"指骄横的匈奴，译文用模糊法将其译成 all，指眼前所有的敌人，利于凸显 terminate 的气势。"名王侍"指古代少数民族声名显赫的王的侍从，表明将军要灭的不只是匈奴王侍从的决心。然而，其译文 Not just the chieftain subjugate 意为不只是匈奴王投降，虽与原文字面义不同，但其本质都是指包括王和侍从在内的整个军团。

4. 既失大军援，遂婴穹庐耻。
　　少小蒙汉恩，何堪坐思此。

译文：But in need he received no aid; To surrender there he was made.

He'd been favored by Han since young; With such a disgrace he was stung.

赏析：与上文一样，译文以句组内押韵的方式去对等原文句组间尾韵的修辞手法。"婴"指缠绕，在文中指李将军因无大军援助而被迫投降，从此背负上了投降游牧民族的耻辱，而译文 To surrender there he was made，体现了李陵投降的不得已。"穹庐"指古代游牧民族居住的毡帐，在译文中和"耻"字一同被省略，但其体现的投降的不情愿感，与 he was made 一致，形式不等但体现的感受一致。"此"为代词，代指上文提到的"穹庐耻"，译者把原文隐性的词义显性化，译成 such a disgrace。

5. **深衷欲有报，投躯未能死。**

   引领望子卿，非君谁相理。

译文：His Majesty's grace he'd repay；He'd die for that to have his day.

He raised his eyes towards Wu Su：Who can understand me now，who?

赏析：原文的句组间尾韵对应译文的句组内尾韵，译文的尾韵密度更高。"报"指报效朝廷，译文将其译成 repay，并用增译法添加了"报"的宾语 His Majesty's grace，即皇上的恩德，以皇帝来代指整个朝廷。"投躯未能死"写的是战斗的结果，即舍身未死，但译文 He'd die for that to have his day 写的是战斗的意愿，即舍身欲死，体现了译者的"再创造"策略，两者都能体现李陵对朝廷的忠心。"引领望"指伸颈远望，译文 He raised his eyes towards 还原了伸颈与远望的姿势。"子卿"指苏武，字子卿，天汉元年奉命以中郎将持节出使匈奴，被扣留 19 年持节不屈，译文直译其原名 Wu Su。译文用冒号译出了"引领望子卿"与"非君谁相理"之间的逻辑关系，属显性化策略。

3.3 老 将 行

3.3.1 诗歌背景

唐玄宗开元二十五年(737 年)，王维奉命出使边塞，在凉州河西节度使副使崔希逸的幕下任节度判官，并度过了一年的军旅生活。在任期间，他深入了解士兵的生活，发现军队中也存在诸多问题，而这首诗就是以老将为例，来反映许多士兵功勋卓著，但最终沦落为无功被弃，被迫以躬耕叫卖为生的结局。《老将行》揭露了军队赏罚蒙昧的不公，也歌颂了老将不计恩怨和精忠报国的节操。

3.3.2 古诗原文

老 将 行

少年十五二十时，
步行夺得胡马骑。
射杀山中白额虎，
肯数邺下黄须儿。
一身转战三千里，
一剑曾当百万师。
汉兵奋迅如霹雳，
虏骑崩腾畏蒺藜。
卫青不败由天幸，
李广无功缘数奇。
自从弃置便衰朽，
世事蹉跎成白首。
昔时飞箭无全目，
今日垂杨生左肘。
路旁时卖故侯瓜，
门前学种先生柳。
苍茫古木连穷巷，
寥落寒山对虚牖。
誓令疏勒出飞泉，
不似颍川空使酒。
贺兰山下阵如云，
羽檄交驰日夕闻。
节使三河募年少，
诏书五道出将军。
试拂铁衣如雪色，

聊持宝剑动星文。

愿得燕弓射大将，

耻令越甲鸣吾君。

莫嫌旧日云中守，

犹堪一战取功勋。

3.3.3 古诗译文

An Old General

When fifteen, twenty or so, a young one,

On foot, I could catch a horse from a Hun.

In hills I'd shoot tigers with a white head;

Is the rash boy from Yeh the best, as said?

For a thousand miles I've fought for the Lord;

I could brave a million troops with my sword.

So fast like thunder the Han soldiers sped;

The cavalrymen fell as thorns they tread.

Blue Watch won, who was helped by Heaven great;

Broad Lee lost, as was haunted by ill fate.

Thrown on the scrapheap, I grew weak in plight;

With the elapse of time, my hair's turned white.

With eyes shut, a target I'd shoot of yore;

Now my left arm aches like a tumor sore.

I'd sell melons by a road like the mean;

Or by my door plant gleeful willows green.

My poor lane sees pines and cypresses old;

My window faces the bleak mountains cold.

I swear to make Shule's spring spurt again,

Not like General Kuan, who drank in vain.

The soldiers at Mt. Holan swarm like cloud;

Urgent orders rush day and night, so loud.

Envoys urge the army to recruit more;

Edits start generals to march to the fore.

The general strokes his mail to shine like snow;

The seven stars on his sword seem to glow.

I'd have a Yan bow to shoot the foes awed;

Ne'er to let armored Huns frighten our Lord.

The deposed general is now coming back;

He will glorify our land with one smack.

（赵彦春　译）

◎ 注释

1. Hun：one of barbaric nomadic Asian people who frequently invaded China, a general term referring to all northern or western invaders or aliens. 胡

2. Yeh：one of the eight most famous capitals in Chinese history, in today's Linchang County, Hopei Province. 邺下

3. Han：China or Chinese, an metonymy adopted because of the powerful Han Empire founded by Pang Liu, King of Han before he won the war and reunified China. 汉

4. Blue Watch：Blue Watch (? -106 B. C.), Ch'ing Wei if transliterated, a renowned commander in the Western Han Dynasty. 卫青

5. Broad Lee：Broad Li (? -119 B. C.), Kuang Li if transliterated, a renowned general fighting against the Huns in the Han Dynasty. 李广

6. gleeful willows：an allusion to Lord Glee, that is, Poolbright T'ao (352 A. D. - 427 A. D.), a verse writer, poet, and litterateur in the Chin Dynasty, and the founder of Chinese idyll, who was once the magistrate of P'engtse. Pure and loft, T'ao resigned from official life several times to live a life of simplicity. There were five willow trees planted in front of his house, so he called himself Mr. Five Willows. 先生柳

7. Shule：name of an old kingdom, in today's Kashgar, New Land (Hsinchiang). 疏勒

8. General Kuan：Fu Kuan (? -131B. C.), an official and general in the Western Han Dynasty. 颍川

9. Mt. Holan：a mountain on the border between Ninghsia and Inner Mongolia. 贺兰山

10. Yan：the State of Yan（1，044 B. C. -222 B. C.），a vassal state in the Spring and Autumn Period，one of the Seven Powers in the Warring States Period. 燕

3.3.4 译文赏析

1. 射杀山中白额虎，肯数邺下黄须儿。
  一身转战三千里，一剑曾当百万师。

译文：In hills I'd shoot tigers with a white head；Is the rash boy from Yeh the best，as said？

For a thousand miles I've fought for the Lord；I could brave a million troops with my sword.

赏析：原文虽然缺少押韵，但采用了用词重复和词义对偶的修辞手法，如"一身"和"一剑"塑造了孤胆英雄的形象，方位词"中"对"下"，颜色词"白"对"黄"，数量词"三千"对"百万"。译文则通过增添句组内尾韵和再现数量词对偶的修辞，来体现诗性。"邺下"位于河北临漳邺镇，古时称为邺城，献帝建安时，曹操据守邺城，因该地名不具备明显的字面义，其译文 Yeh 采用了音译法。"黄须儿"指曹操的次子曹彰，彰绰号黄须儿，奋勇破敌，却功归诸将，译文 the rash boy 译出其字面义，而外国读者对其引申的典故，则要依赖注解。

2. 汉兵奋迅如霹雳，虏骑崩腾畏蒺藜。

译文：So fast like thunder the Han soldiers sped；
  The cavalrymen fell as thorns they tread.

赏析：原文与译文同押尾韵。"蒺藜"是果实有三角刺的植物，这里指战地所用障碍物——铁蒺藜，译文 thorns 采用模糊法，用上义词"刺"来象征其子类"铁蒺藜"，抹去了"蒺藜"所关联的植物含义。译文的另一个特点是采用过去时，利于 speed 的过去式与 tread 形成尾韵。

3. 卫青不败由天幸，李广无功缘数奇。

译文：Blue Watch won，who was helped by Heaven great；
  Broad Lee lost，as was haunted by ill fate.

赏析：原文"幸"与"奇"的元音押韵，译文 great 与 fate 押尾韵。原文的"不"与"无"同

为否定词，在词义和位置上对偶，而译文则采用反义词 won 与 lost，并在每句的第三个字的位置上形成对偶。"卫青"指汉代名将，因征伐匈奴而官至大将军，是汉武帝皇后卫子夫之弟，其译文 Blue Watch 采用字面译法和英文名的格式，其中"青"最为讲究。根据先秦荀子《劝学》："青，取之于蓝，而青于蓝"，可见青色是一种发绿的蓝色，因此译为 Blue。

4. **自从弃置便衰朽，世事蹉跎成白首。**

   昔时飞箭无全目，今日垂杨生左肘。

译文：Thrown on the scrapheap, I grew weak in plight; With the elapse of time, my
　　　　hair's turned white.

　　　　With eyes shut, a target I'd shoot of yore; Now my left arm aches like a tumor
　　　　sore.

赏析：原文的诗性在于句子尾韵和句首词义对偶，而译文在于句组内的尾韵。原文四句写了老将被遗弃后的清苦生活。"飞箭无全目"指射箭能击中雀的眼睛，使雀双目不全，以体现射艺之精湛。为了押尾韵，该句译文将"昔时"调整到末尾，并译成非基本词 yore。"垂杨"以"杨"谐"疡"（疮），指老将久不习武，如同左臂生了疡瘤，译文 tumor sore 显性化了其比喻义。

5. **路旁时卖故侯瓜，门前学种先生柳。**

译文：I'd sell melons by a road like the mean;

　　　　Or by my door plant gleeful willows green.

赏析：原文无尾韵，诗性在于词义对偶，如方位词"门前"对"路旁"，而译文在于尾韵。"故侯"，指秦东陵侯邵平，秦破后，沦为布衣，以种瓜于长安东城为生，与老将遭遇类似，其译文省略了故侯的典故，再现了老将路边以卖瓜为生的情景。"先生柳"指陶渊明弃官归隐后，因门前有五株杨柳，遂自号"五柳先生"，与老将遭遇类似，而其译文也采用减译法，省略了典故，保留了字面义。外国读者在理解 gleeful willows 对"五柳先生"的象征意义时，需要依赖注解。

6. **誓令疏勒出飞泉，不似颍川空使酒。**

译文：I swear to make Shule's spring spurt again,

　　　　Not like General Kuan, who drank in vain.

赏析：原文的特点是用典。"疏勒"指汉疏勒城，后汉耿恭与匈奴在此作战，匈奴于城下断绝其水源，恭于城中打井，但至十五丈犹不得水，向井祈祷后，终得泉水。因字面喻义不详，译者采用音译法，再现了地名的音，并增译了 again 以形成尾韵。"颍川"指前汉颍川人灌夫，为人刚直，解除军职之后，牢骚酗酒，后被诛。其译文 General Kuan 再现了"灌夫"的名与职务，也代替了地名"颍川"，译出了其所指义。"空"字的译文 in vain 不仅译出了"灌夫"使酒的徒劳与空虚，而且与上句形成尾韵。原文和译文用"疏勒"和"颍川"的典故来表明老将并未意志消沉，而是仍然想和后汉名将一样，与战士同甘共苦，为国立功。

第二部分　田园诗

第四章 参禅悟道

4.1 赠焦道士

4.1.1 诗歌背景

《赠焦道士》为王维在济州(今属山东济宁)任职期间所作,地近东岳泰山。焦道士,即焦炼师,长期居于嵩山。整首诗通过列举各种典故、道术,来体现焦道士的见识广博和道法高深,并表达了诗人对焦道士的敬仰。全诗引用了许多神话故事、人物、自然景观、仙术,如三岛、八公、一壶、缩地、玉童、割酒、分风、天老、行气、养空、鸿濛,来比喻焦道士的道术精湛和诗人的敬仰。全诗尾韵特点鲜明,12 句中有 6 句末尾同时押韵,如公、中、童、风、空、濛都带后鼻音,而译文 12 分句间均双双押尾韵。

4.1.2 古诗原文

赠焦道士

海上游三岛,

淮南预八公。

坐知千里外,

跳向一壶中。

缩地朝珠阙,

行天使玉童。

饮人聊割酒，

送客乍分风。

天老能行气，

吾师不养空。

谢君徒雀跃，

无可问鸿濛。

4.1.3 古诗译文

To Master Chiao, the Wordist

You surf to Three Isles on the blue

And meet in Huainan Eight Men true.

Shut in, you know all, where and what;

To rise, you jump into a pot.

Shrinking distance, to court you fly,

And order sprites to cruise the sky.

Toasting, you cleft the cup and brew;

To guests, you split wind into two.

Like Sky Old, you run air employed;

You need not contemplate the void.

Like a sparrow you leap ahead,

No need to ask Blackgoose instead.

（赵彦春　译）

◎ 注释

1. Three Isles: referring to the three fairy islands in East Sea, which is called East China Sea now, more than 700,000 square kilometers. 三岛

2. Huainan: an area in the drainage basin of the Huai River, first an eastern barbarian area governed by a vassal state of Chough called Choulai in the Western Chough Period,

enfeoffed as Kingdom of Huainan in the Han Dynasty. 淮南

3. Eight Men true：eight alchemists invited by King of Huainan. When they arrived，the porter was disappointed at their old age and would not admit them. The eight men said："You discriminate our age，now we'll be young." So saying，they turned into children. King of Huainan，so surprised，bowed to them as their disciple. The eight men could make all kinds of miracles，and later rose to the Heavens，taking King of Huainan with them. 八公

4. Sky Old：Lord Yellow's advisor as is recorded in *Bamboo Book Annals* and *Lord Yellow Cartshaft*. 天老

5. Blackgoose：an immortal in Sir Lush's fable，who seems to know nothing but leaping happily. 鸿濛

4.1.4　译文赏析

1. 海上游三岛，淮南预八公。
　　坐知千里外，跳向一壶中。

译文：You surf to Three Isles on the blue；And meet in Huainan Eight Men true.
　　　Shut in，you know all，where and what；To rise，you jump into a pot.

赏析："三岛"指海上的三座神山，分别为蓬莱、瀛洲、方丈，相传为神仙所居之处，其译文 Three Isles 以大写来强调岛的特殊性。"预"通"遇"。"淮南预八公"谓焦道士在淮南加入"八公"的行列，已成仙，其译文 Eight Men 以大写来表达"八公"的特指性，并增译 true 来与 blue 形成尾韵。因"八公"文化的互文性较高，因此目标语读者对其理解要基于注解。"跳向一壶中"源自《方术列传》，相传市中有老翁卖药，与费长房俱入壶中，惟见玉堂严丽，旨酒甘肴，后长房欲求神术。诗人用此事，谓焦道士乃仙人。To rise 为增译，与前句 Shut in 结构对称。"跳向一壶中"的理解要基于典故，难以概括在字里行间，因此译者直译其字面义，并将"千里外"的事译成 where and what，与 pot 形成尾韵。

2. 缩地朝珠阙，行天使玉童。

译文：Shrinking distance，to court you fly，
　　　And order sprites to cruise the sky.

赏析："缩地"指缩地之术，源自《壶公传》"费长房有神术，能缩地脉⋯⋯"。"珠阙"指用珍珠宝贝做的宫殿，诗中指长安天子的宫殿。"玉童"指仙童，sprites 指小精灵，两者

身形相似，且都会法术。前句增译 fly，与后句 sky 形成尾韵，而且 to court you fly 与 to cruise the sky 在句法和音节上对偶。

3. 饮人聊割酒，送客作分风。

译文：Toasting, you cleft the cup and brew;

　　　　To guests, you split wind into two.

赏析："割酒"源自《左慈》，相传左慈与曹操分别，慈用簪子将杯中酒一分为二，自己喝一半，但曹操没喝另一半。左慈喝完酒后，把杯子抛向房梁，杯子如飞鸟一般悬浮在半空中，在坐者无不翘首。toasting 体现了场景，cleft the cup 译出了"割酒"的字义，brew 是为了与 two 押尾韵而增译的成分，也能体现焦道士的法术。"分风"指神仙将风分为两个方向，诗中借指送客分离。

4. 天老能行气，吾师不养空。

译文：Like Sky Old, you run air employed;

　　　　You need not contemplate the void.

赏析："天老"相传为黄帝辅臣。"行气"是指道教中的一种以呼吸吐纳为主的养生内修方法，以延年益寿。译文 Sky Old、run air 均译出了源语的字面义，其文化内涵的理解需依赖注解。"养空"指修养其空虚之性，以避免被俗累所羁绊。译文 You need not contemplate the void 译出了"不"字的准确深意，即"不需"，而非"不做"。译文 void 可指空间和心理上的虚空，与原文心灵上的"空"字对等。

4.2　赠东岳焦炼师

4.2.1　诗歌背景

《赠东岳焦炼师》为王维在济州(今属山东济宁)任职期间所作，地近东岳泰山。整首诗赞扬了焦炼师阅历广博、道术精湛和闻名于世，并表达了诗人对焦炼师的敬仰。全诗引用了许多典故和神话故事，并用许多具体的物品比喻焦炼师道术精湛和皇帝的赏识。描写炼师、禅师隐居深山，闭关修道，是王维田园诗中一大重要的子类。整首诗的译文体现了译者不拘于语言形式，但忠于源语写作目的、深层语义的特点。

4.2.2　古诗原文

赠东岳焦炼师

先生千岁馀，

五岳遍曾居。

遥识齐侯鼎，

新过王母庐。

不能师孔墨，

何事问长沮。

玉管时来凤，

铜盘即钓鱼。

竦身空里语，

明目夜中书。

自有还丹术，

时论太素初。

频蒙露版诏，

时降软轮车。

山静泉逾响，

松高枝转疏。

支颐问樵客，

世上复何如。

4.2.3　古诗译文

To Great Master Chiao on Mt. East

Master, you're a thousand years old,

Having lived in Five Mounts, as told.

Marquis of Ch'i's tripod you've seen,

And to Queen Mother's lodge you've been.

As you won't do Confucius' task,

The worldly way you need not ask.

Your flute lures phoenixes to stay;

With a copper plate fish you may.

If rising, you can wing your flight,

And read at midnight without light.

You know how cinnabar's refined,

And talk on the birth of mankind.

Your act's moved His Majesty's heart;

He'd treat you to a cushioned cart.

Mountains quiet, the spring louder flows;

Leafage sparse, the pine taller grows.

You ask a woodman, propped your chin:

"What's happened to the worldly din?"

（赵彦春　译）

◎ 注释

1. Five Mounts: the Five Mountains in China, including Mount Ever in Shanhsi, Mount Scale in Hunan, Mount Arch in Shantung, Mount Flora in Sha'anhsi, and Mount Tower in Honan, which symbolizes the unity of the Chinese nation from north, south, east, west and center. 五岳

2. Queen Mother: referring to Mother West, a sovereign goddess living on Mt. Queen in Chinese myths. She was originally described as human-bodied, tiger-toothed, leopard-tailed and hoopoe-haired, regarded as a goddess in charge of women protection, marriage and procreation, and longevity. According to *Sir Lush*, with the Word, Queen Mother sat on Mt. Young Broad. 王母

3. Confucius: Confucius (551 B. C. -479 B. C.), a renowned thinker, educator and statesman in the Spring and Autumn Period, born in the State of Lu, who was the founder of Confucianism and who had exerted profound influence on Chinese culture. 孔

4. Phoenixes：in Chinese myths，phoenixes，auspicious birds，unlike ordinary ones，only perch on parasol trees. 凤

5. cinnabar：raw material for elixir in Wordist alchemy. 还丹

6. pine：a symbol of longevity and rectitude in Chinese culture. 松

4.2.4　译文赏析

1. 赠东岳焦炼师

译文： To Great Master Chiao on Mt. East

赏析："五岳"为中国五大名山的总称，分别为东岳泰山、西岳华山、中岳嵩山、北岳恒山、南岳衡山。诗中"东岳"指泰山，是中国古代道教、帝王封禅的圣地。其译文 Mt. East 直译了其古代的称呼，而非现代的 Mt. Taishan，以保留诗的古风。"炼师"为道士的敬称，喻义德高思精，其译文 Great Master 在表达敬称的功能上与原文对等。

2. 遥识齐侯鼎，新过王母庐。

译文： Marquis of Ch'i's tripod you've seen,

And to Queen Mother's lodge you've been.

赏析："齐侯鼎"指带有"齐侯"铭文的青铜礼器，古代把鼎作为立国重器，其译文 Marquis of Ch'i's tripod 覆盖了原文的字面义"齐侯的三足鼎"。"王母庐"指山东泰山脚下的王母池，相传是西王母召集群仙的地方，在唐朝被称为瑶池，后为了与昆仑山瑶池区别，改称为王母池。其译文 Queen Mother's lodge 译出了"王母"的字面义，"庐"本意为沿途迎候宾客的房舍，其译文 lodge 指供打猎者居住的乡间小屋，与该词意象一致。

3. 不能师孔墨，何事问长沮。

译文： As you won't do Confucius' task,

The worldly way you need not ask.

赏析："孔墨"指孔子和墨子，在此诗中比喻效法儒家思想的责任，因此译为 Confucius' task。"长沮"指春秋时楚国的一位隐士，孔子曾偶遇正在躬耕的长沮，并向其问路。译文 The worldly way 虽然抹去了"长沮"的字眼，但用 worldly（尘世间）保留了其归隐脱俗的喻义。两句意为焦炼师若不能效法孔墨，也就无须奔波四方、向人问路了。

4. 玉管时来凤，铜盘即钓鱼。

译文： Your flute lures phoenixes to stay;

With a copper plate fish you may.

赏析： "玉管"指箫。《列仙传》："秦穆公……善吹箫，能致孔雀、白鹤于庭。""铜盘即钓鱼"源自《后汉书·方术列传》，用于比喻从铜盘中引鱼而出的仙术。译者运用倒装手法将 you may fish 调整为 fish you may，不仅有文学风格，而且能与上句增译的 stay 形成尾韵。诗人用"玉管"和"铜盘"来比喻焦炼师有神术，因此两句主语都为 you。

5. 竦身空里语，明目夜中书。

自有还丹术，时论太素初。

译文： If rising, you can wing your flight, And read at midnight without light.

You know how cinnabar's refined, And talk on the birth of mankind.

赏析： "竦身"指纵身向上跳，遂入云中，指轻功，"竦"通"耸"。"明目夜中书"指炼师目明，能在夜间写字。虽然 read 与"书"字义不同，但都能体现出焦炼师的目明，体现了译者不拘泥于表现形式，而忠于深层义和写作目的。"空里语"指坐空虚之中，与人言语，在译文中被弱化，you can wing your flight 省略了"语"字，体现了译者不拘于形式，而忠于表现焦炼师轻功精湛的写作目的，其语言形式采用了创译策略。"还丹术"指道家炼丹之术，因朱砂是炼丹和长生不老药的原料之一，其译文 cinnabar's refined 体现了朱砂提炼的过程。"太素"指古代最原始的物质，古人在《列子·天瑞》中记载，物质世界是按照虚无、气、形态、物质的顺序而逐渐产生的。"太素初"的译文 the birth of mankind 为求押尾韵，将"物质的诞生"译成"人类的诞生"，两者都能表达万物伊始的语义，体现了译者不拘于形而忠于义的特点。

6. 频蒙露版诏，时降软轮车。

译文： Your act's moved His Majesty's heart;

He'd treat you to a cushioned cart.

赏析： "露版"即露布，不缄封的文书，指奏章，在诗中体现皇帝对焦炼师频繁的征召。其译文 moved His Majesty's heart 虽然抹去了诏书的字眼，但呈现了"频蒙露版"的喻义，即焦炼师的名气引起了皇帝的注意。"软轮车"指为使车不致颠簸，以蒲草包裹车轮，古时征召有众望之人，用"软轮车"以示礼敬，其译文 cushioned cart 再现了马车的安稳性。

4.3　过乘如禅师萧居士嵩丘兰若

4.3.1　诗歌背景

　　这首诗作于王维在嵩山隐居期间(开元二十二年(734 年)秋至开元二十三年(735 年)春)。王维隐居嵩山期间,与山上修行佛法的两兄弟交好,所以作此诗赠予他们。全诗通过动态的刻画,如"鸣磬""行踏空林""落叶声",描写了禅师的日常生活和朴素宁静的精神面貌。通过对雨水、家具的描写,来体现禅师住处的简陋和修行的境界,如"迸水""香案""雨花""石床"。禅师在简陋的居住条件中找到了修行的乐趣,其禅境已接近天竺国归来的高僧,令诗人敬佩不已。

4.3.2　古诗原文

过乘如禅师萧居士嵩丘兰若

无著天亲弟与兄,
嵩丘兰若一峰晴。
食随鸣磬巢乌下,
行踏空林落叶声。
迸水定侵香案湿,
雨花应共石床平。
深洞长松何所有,
俨然天竺古先生。

4.3.3　古诗译文

A Visit to Buddhist Hsiao Called Zen Master
Yana at Grove Calm on Mt. Tower

Non Fame and Sky Dear are two brothers fine;

Mt. Tower and Grove Calm face the peak in shine.

The crows fly down for food at chime stone sound,

Stirring leaves from the trees to fall aground.

Water is splashed to the incense, there spread,

Like flowers rained to all, even the stone bed.

How is the tall pine there by the deep cave?

Much like Master Old from India, so grave.

（赵彦春　译）

◎ 注释

1. Zen：a kind of performance of quietude in a form of meditation or contemplation. When Sanskrit jana was spread to China, it was translated as zan or zen for this kind of practice. 禅

2. Grove Calm：a grove good for meditation. 兰若

3. Mt. Tower：located in the west of present-day Honan Province, one of the Five Mountains in Chinese culture. 嵩丘

4. Non Fame：name of a Bodhisattva. 无著

5. Sky Dear：name of a Bodhisattva. 天亲

6. flowers rained：a shower of flowers like thorn apples or angel's trumpets. 雨花

7. pine：a symbol of longevity and rectitude in Chinese culture. 松

8. Master Old from India：referring to Buddha in this poem. 古先生

4.3.4　译文赏析

1. 过乘如禅师萧居士嵩丘兰若

译文：A Visit to Buddhist Hsiao Called Zen Master Yana at Grove Calm on Mt. Tower

赏析：题中的"禅师"是对和尚的敬称，译为 Zen Master。"乘如"为法号，梵语的读音为 Yana，指运载工具，喻义佛法济渡众生。"居士"是在家修行佛法的人，因此译为 Buddhist。"兰若"也是佛教名词，"若"念 rě，梵名 Aranya，字面义为森林，喻义远离人间的寂静处，常被古人用于代指寺庙，因此被译成地名 Grove Calm。

2. 食随鸣磬巢鸟下，行路空林落叶声。

译文：The crows fly down for food at chime stone sound,

Stirring leaves from the trees to fall aground.

赏析："鸣磬(pán)"指佛教的打击乐器，形似钵，用石或玉制成，因此译为 chime stone sound。"巢乌"指筑巢的乌鸦，其译文 The crows fly down 省略了"巢"，增译了 fly down，使译文画面更有动态感。译文 Stirring leaves from the trees to fall aground 减译了"行踏"，着重描写了"林"和"落叶"，并用系表结构 fall aground 收尾，以形成尾韵。

3. 迸水定侵香案湿，雨花应共石床平。

译文：Water is splashed to the incense, there spread,

　　　Like flowers rained to all, even the stone bed.

赏析："迸水"指高处泻落的水，译为句子 Water is splashed。"香案"为放置香炉的条桌，译文 the incense 减译了"案"。"雨花"指雨滴溅起的水花打在"石床"上，译文中 all 和 even 体现了对禅师住所"何等简陋"的感叹。在此等陋室中，禅师仍然能找到修行的乐趣，体现了其精神境界之高。

4. 深洞长松何所有，俨然天竺古先生。

译文：How is the tall pine there by the deep cave?

　　　Much like Master Old from India, so grave.

赏析："古先生"指老子，据《西升经》，老子西至天竺为佛，号古先生。其译文 Master Old 直译尊称"古先生"的字面义，而非实指人 Lao Tzu，属于异化策略，保留了原文内容的特点。"深洞"和"俨然"被分别译成地点状语 by the deep cave 和感叹词 so grave，置于句尾，以形成尾韵。

第五章 做客田园

5.1 济州过赵叟家宴

5.1.1 诗歌背景

此诗作于王维在济州任司仓参军时(开元十年(722年)至开元十三年(725年)间)。诗人去赵老家赴宴,很欣赏赵老的隐居生活,故作此诗。这首诗描写了一位久居城里的官员赵老,得空到乡间闭门隐居,说的是儒道的事,吃的是自种的农家菜,住的是斜阳高柳为伴的农家院,令诗人由衷地向往起优雅的田园生活。

5.1.2 古诗原文

济州过赵叟家宴

虽与人境接,

闭门成隐居。

道言庄叟事,

儒行鲁人馀。

深巷斜晖静,

闲门高柳疏。

荷锄修药圃,

散帙曝农书。

上客摇芳翰，

中厨馈野蔬。

夫君第高饮，

景晏出林间。

5.1.3 古诗译文

Visiting Chao in Chichow

Although close to the worldly din,

You are a recluse once shut in.

In the Word, with Sir Lush you talk;

For rituals, with Lu Man you walk.

The deep lane receives afterglow;

The high gate sees willows droop low.

You farm curing herbs with a hoe,

And read farm books, loose your hair-do.

To guests you waves your writing brush

And in your kitchen cook greens lush.

O in great altitude you drink;

Of immortals you are the pink

(赵彦春 译)

◎ 注释

1. Chichow: it refers to a city in ancient China, and is called Heze in Shandong Province nowadays. 济州

2. the Word: referring to Tao if transliterated, the most significant and profoundest concept in Chinese philosophy. According to Laocius's *The Word and the World*: "The Word is void, but its use is infinite. O deep! It seems to be the root of all things." 道言

3. Sir Lush: Chuangtsu if transliterated, an important philosopher in the Warring States Period,

one of the representatives of Wordism (Taoism). One of the most important Chinese classics is *Sir Lush*, philosophical fables written by Sir Lush. 庄叟

4. Lu Man：referring to Confucius (551 B. C. -479 B. C.) from Lu. Confucius was a renowned thinker, educator and statesman in the Spring and Autumn Period, born in the State of Lu, and as the founder of Confucianism, he has exerted profound influence on Chinese culture. 鲁人

5.1.4 译文赏析

1. 虽与人境接，闭门成隐居。
道言庄叟事，儒行鲁人馀。

译文：Although close to the worldly din, You are a recluse once shut in.

In the Word, with Sir Lush you talk; For rituals, with Lu Man you walk.

赏析：原文两句组间形成尾韵，而译者一如既往地将尾韵修辞体现在句组内。"人境"指尘世间人居住的地方，诗中指赵姓老人住得离城市不远，其译文 worldly din 体现了尘世的喧嚣。第1、2分句通过 although 形成了主从句结构，共用主语 you。"道言"指道教的学说、经典。"庄叟"指庄子，"叟"为老人。"儒行"指合乎儒教的言行，而"鲁人馀"指鲁国人孔子的遗风。译文 In the Word... 与 For rituals... 在句法上结构完全对偶，字数一致，分别体现了赵老在"言"和"行"上的高尚，属于音、形、义对等的高质量译文。

2. 深巷斜晖静，闲门高柳疏。
荷锄修药圃，散帙曝农书。

译文：The deep lane receives afterglow; The high gate sees willows droop low.

You farm curing herbs with a hoe, And read farm books, loose your hair-do.

赏析："斜晖"指傍晚西斜的阳光，落日余晖。"闲门"指进出人数不多的门，诗中指门庭清闲。"高"在诗中易产生歧义，一种是"门高"，另一种是"高柳"，译者选择前者，译文 The high gate sees willows droop low 再现了源语的意象，即"门"和"柳"，但意象的描写方式与源语不同，具有一定创译性。"帙(zhì)"指帛书用囊盛放，用于装套的线装书，书一套叫做一帙，后也指书画外面包着的套子。译文 And read farm books, loose your hair-do 再现了读农书的内容，虽减译了"帙"字，但增译了 loose your hair-do 以体现赵老农忙后回书屋休息的过程，并利于形成尾韵。

3. 上客摇芳翰，中厨馈野蔬。

译文：To guests you waves your writing brush; And in your kitchen cook greens lush.

赏析："上客"指尊贵的宾客。"芳翰(hàn)"指带芬芳的笔和墨，是对别人书画作品的敬称，被译为 writing brush。"中厨"指内厨房。"野蔬"为野菜，诗中指自种的各类蔬菜，被译为 greens lush。为了让 brush 和 lush 位于句尾以形成尾韵，译者巧妙地将状语 To guests 前置，并将形容词 lush 后置在名词 greens 的右侧。

5.2　韦给事山居

5.2.1　诗歌背景

韦家是唐代非常显赫的世家，在当时亲近皇权，具有极高的社会地位。"给事"指给事中，是门下省的重要职位，在唐代是伴随皇帝左右的近臣。韦给事为自己修建了一座山居，在日常工作之余，能在山水田园间有情调地小憩一番。全诗以山居环境的优雅来烘托出韦给事的显贵，在内容上主要描写了山居的环境，如山壑的壮阔和林间的情调。全诗尾韵特点明显，四组句的末尾均押同一音韵，即曾、登、藤、能，其译文尾韵的处理技巧，体现了译者对英文词性灵巧的运用。

5.2.2　古诗原文

韦给事山居

幽寻得此地，

讵有一人曾。

大壑随阶转，

群山入户登。

庖厨出深竹，

印绶隔垂藤。

即事辞轩冕，

谁云病未能。

5.2.3　古诗译文

The Cottage of Wei, an Imperial Inspector

I've found this place as I explore;

Travelers visiting there'd be more.

Following the steps, you see dales great;

The mountains would enter the gate.

A kitchen's found in bamboo deep;

Rattan vines o'er their ribbons sweep.

When giving up positions fat,

Who will say it's hard to do that?

（赵彦春　译）

◎ 注释

1. bamboo：a symbol of integrity and altitude, one of the four most important images in Chinese literature, which are wintersweet, orchid, bamboo, and chrysanthemum. 竹

2. rattan vines：it refers to a plant, which symbolizes that the officials forgot their official identity in the pastoral life. 垂藤

3. ribbons：it refers to the ribbons on seal or stamp, which can symbolize official position. 印绶

4. positions fat：it refers to high official positions or distinguished nobles, symbolized by their cart and formal hat. 轩冕

5.2.4　译文赏析

1. *幽寻得此地，讵有一人曾*。

译文：I've found this place as I explore;

Travelers visiting there'd be more.

赏析："幽寻"指静悄悄地寻找，诗中指在幽静的地方找到一处地方。"讵"中的"巨"指所有的事，言字旁指谈论，合并后指谈论任何事物，在诗中意为"据说"。为了与前句的explore 形成尾韵，译者将"一人"译成 more 和虚拟语气 there'd be，以"将有更多人"译"曾有一人"。

2. **大壑随阶转，群山入户登**。

译文：Following the steps, you see dales great;

The mountains would enter the gate.

赏析："大壑"指巨大的沟壑、峡谷。其译文 dales great 将形容词 great 置于名词 dales 的后方，以便与 gate 形成尾韵。根据其他诗歌译文的尾韵，可见译者形成尾韵的常用技巧为形容词、动词后置。"群山入户登"为拟人的比喻，描写了群山似乎要登门入户，因此译者采用虚拟语气 would。

3. **庖厨出深竹，印绶隔垂藤**。

译文：A kitchen's found in bamboo deep;

Rattan vines o'er their ribbons sweep.

赏析："庖厨"指厨房或厨师。"印绶"指印信的丝带，用于将印信佩戴在身边，在诗中比喻官爵。"印绶隔垂藤"字面指垂藤隔着官员身上佩戴的"印绶"，其深意是比喻在田园之乐中，人们将身份、地位都放在一边。"深竹"与"印绶"的译文 bamboo deep 和 ribbons sweep 也体现了译者形成尾韵的常用技巧为形容词、动词后置。

5.3　韦侍郎山居

5.3.1　诗歌背景

《韦侍郎山居》作于开元二十五年（737 年）春。韦侍郎指韦济，唐郑州阳武（今原阳县）人。韦济少年时以能文知名，与杜甫、高适有交往。开元初，韦济为鄄城令，后又历任冯翊太守、户部侍郎、尚书左丞、尚书户部等官职。《韦侍郎山居》描写了久居尘世的韦侍郎空闲时与好友一同隐居山水花鸟之间，待小憩之后又回朝料理国家大政。诗中的闲花、岩谷、瀑水、杉松、啼鸟、归涧、归云、抱峰、夔龙体现了大自然的情趣不输于宫中的乐器。诗中押韵以 ABAB 结构的尾韵为主，如踪、松、峰、龙、钟、容。

5.3.2 古诗原文

韦侍郎山居

幸忝君子顾，
遂陪尘外踪。
闲花满岩谷，
瀑水映杉松。
啼鸟忽归涧，
归云时抱峰。
良游盛簪绂，
继迹多夔龙。
讵枉青门道，
胡闻长乐钟。
清晨去朝谒，
车马何从容。

5.3.3 古诗译文

To the Cottage of Wei, a Ministerial Aide

I stroll with you out of the world,
So favored I feel at your call.
Free flowers bloom all over the dale,
The pines splashed by the waterfall.
Some warblers fly down to the creek,
The peaks by homing clouds entwined.
There cloud companions' hats and caps

Followed by unicorns behind.

How can we let down Blue Gate Way?

Here we can hear a long-life toll.

Tomorrow we'll go see our Lord；

How gracefully our carts will roll!

（赵彦春 译）

◎ 注释

1. hats and caps：they refer to the hairpin and hat ribbon to fix the hat for ancient officials to their head. 簪绂

2. unicorn：a divine animal，a symbol of loyal minister in Chinese culture. The snake-shaped animal shouts like thunder，shines like moon and sun，and summons wind and rain in water (*The Classic of Mountains and Rivers*). Its image frequently appears on the bronze relics from Shang and Zhou Dynasties. 夔龙

3. Blue Gate Way：the way leading from and to Blue Gate，the southern gate of the three gates on the east wall of Long Peace. 青门道

4. long-life toll：a toll played in emperor's palace whose name implies longevity and happiness. 长乐钟

5.3.4 译文赏析

1. 幸忝君子顾，遂陪尘外踪。

   闲花满岩谷，瀑水映杉松。

译文：I stroll with you out of the world, So favored I feel at your call.

Free flowers bloom all over the dale, The pines splashed by the waterfall.

赏析：原文的尾韵特点是 ABAB 结构，其尾韵的密度比译文高。"尘外"指人间俗尘之外。为形成尾韵，译者将词序的调整跨度扩展到两句之间，将"幸忝"与"遂陪"二句的顺序在译文中互换，体现了译者对译文音韵观察力的广度。"闲花"指野花、幽雅的花，译文用 free 来体现花的野和幽雅性。"映"指通过照射而显现，诗中指以瀑布作背景来衬托出松树的形状，其译文 splashed by 增近了瀑布与松杉树的距离和互动性。

2. 啼鸟忽归涧，归云时抱峰。

译文：Some warblers fly down to the creek,

The peaks by homing clouds entwined.

赏析："啼鸟"指"百舌""黄鹂""青竹笋""戴胜"等能发出悦耳鸣叫的鸟类，其译文 warblers 在西方指莺类，其特性就是能发出悦耳的声音，在物种特性上与原文对等。"涧"指夹在两山间的水沟、小溪，译为 the creek。在两句译文的字里行间，虽然 some 与 home 的音韵最为接近，但句法、词性的约束使其难以在两句的同一平行位置押韵，所以译者选择将动词 entwined 后置，并将状语 by homing clouds 前置，以和 creek 形成尾韵。

3. 良游盛簪绂，继迹多夔龙。

译文：There cloud companions' hats and caps;

Followed by unicorns behind.

赏析："簪绂"指冠簪和缨带，是古代官员用于固定帽子的配饰，常用于比喻显贵的仕宦。其译文 hats and caps 保留了这一比喻过程，而非直译其比喻义。"夔龙"是一种蛇状神兽，根据《山海经·大荒东经》："夔状如牛，苍身而无角，一足，出入水则必有风雨，其光如日月，其声如雷，其名曰夔。"其译文 unicorns 体现了译者采用文化符号对等的策略。因 unicorns 在西方文化里被尊为神兽，译者在对夔龙进行翻译时，将其译成 unicorn。虽然具体的神兽形象不同，但其作为神兽的文化符号和地位是一致的。

4. 讵枉青门道，胡闻长乐钟。

译文：How can we let down Blue Gate Way?

Here we can hear a long-life toll.

赏析：原文为句组间押尾韵，而译文的押韵则落在句组内的头韵。"青门道"指古长安青门外的大道，出自李白的《寓言》，其译文 Blue Gate Way 直译其字面义，并大写以标记地名。其中"青"字容易造成误解，其本义是蓝色、蓝色矿石或草木的颜色，古有"青取之于蓝而胜于蓝"，是一种接近绿色的蓝色，因此译成 Blue。"长乐钟"指汉朝长乐宫的撞钟，"长乐宫"后被用于泛指皇家宫殿，诗中比喻皇宫的钟声。因"长乐钟"指一种乐器，具有可复制性，非专有名词，所以其译文 long-life toll 为小写。"长乐"寓意长寿和长久的快乐，而我国古代统治者更注重"永生文化"，因此译文 long-life toll 减译"乐"而保留"长寿"。

第六章 归山隐居

6.1 纳 凉

6.1.1 诗歌背景

《纳凉》是王维的一首描写景物的五言短诗。诗人通过清流、大川、长风、涟漪、濯足、莲叶等字眼，描绘了一处沁人心脾的纳凉胜地。从字面上，诗人写的是自然景观和人境的融合，但深意上，诗人隐约地表达了自己渴望远离炙热的官场生涯，并隐居于一个理想和清凉的世界里的愿望。全诗的尾韵采用 ABCB 结构，如"中""风""空""躬""翁""东"，译文的尾韵结构与其一致。

6.1.2 古诗原文

纳 凉

乔木万馀株，
清流贯其中。
前临大川口，
豁达来长风。
涟漪涵白沙，
素鲔如游空。

偃卧盘石上，

翻涛沃微躬。

漱流复濯足，

前对钓鱼翁。

贪饵凡几许，

徒思莲叶东。

6.1.3 古诗译文

Enjoying the Cool

There stand myriads of trees so tall，

Through which a limpid river flows.

In front you face the river mouth

So open that a long wind blows.

The ripples carry some white sand

Over which white sturgeons swim free.

On the stone I lie on my back，

While the water splashes to me.

The waves go thru between my feet，

To the fisher and what's near him.

How many fish will bite the bait?

East of the lotus leaves they swim.

(赵彦春 译)

◎ 注释

1. limpid river：it's frequently quoted to symbolize honest and whitehanded officials. 清流

2. open：it refers to open river mouth，which symbolizes the open-mindedness of the poet. 豁达

3. white sturgeons：a large freshwater fish，which swims freely in water as a symbol of the
   poet's freedom. 素鲔

4. lotus：a symbol of purity and elegance in Chinese culture and a common topic in Chinese

literature，unsoiled though out of soil, so clean with all leaves green. 莲

6.1.4　译文赏析

1. 乔木万馀株，清流贯其中。
   前临大川口，豁达来长风。

译文：There stand myriads of trees so tall, Through which a limpid river flows.

In front you face the river mouth, So open that a long wind blows.

赏析：原文尾韵为 ABCB 结构，译文的尾韵结构与原文一致。"乔木"指树身高大的树木，其译文 trees so tall 通过形容词和程度副词来体现这种树的特性，并倒装成句。"清流"字面指清澈的流水，可用于比喻德行高洁的士大夫，其译文 limpid river flows 指清澈的河流，再现了源语的景象。译文 Through which 对应"其中"，连接了两句的逻辑关系，也标记了两句的主从句结构。"豁达"指心胸开阔和性格开朗，诗中指"大川口"，也比喻诗人的心境，其译文 open 可指 open river mouth，也能比喻 open-minded。

2. 涟漪涵白沙，素鲔如游空。
   偃卧盘石上，翻涛沃微躬。

译文：The ripples carry some white sand, Over which white sturgeons swim free.

On the stone I lie on my back, While the water splashes to me.

赏析："素鲔"指鲟鱼，背青碧，腹为白色，其译文 white sturgeons 指白鲟鱼，以鱼的自由来比喻诗人的自由。译文 Over which 为增译部分，显现了两句关系，使得译文更具连贯性。"偃卧"指仰卧，诗中指睡姿，与译文 lie on my back 描述的睡姿一致。"微躬"为卑贱的身子，属于谦词，诗中指诗人自己。"沃"为浇水，其译文 splashes 意为发出声响地泼洒，描绘了拍石浪花溅在诗人身上的田园情趣。为了让读者身临其境，译文采用一般现在时。

3. 漱流复濯足，前对钓鱼翁。
   贪饵凡几许，徒思莲叶东。

译文：The waves go thru between my feet, To the fisher and what's near him.

How many fish will bite the bait? East of the lotus leaves they swim.

赏析：译文的尾韵为 ABAB 结构。"漱流"指用流水漱口，诗中比喻隐居生活。"濯

足"意为洗去脚污，可比喻清除世尘，保持高洁。其译文 The waves go thru between my feet 再现了原文王维浴足于清流间的情景。"贪饵"与"莲叶东"出自汉乐府《江南》的"鱼戏莲叶间……鱼戏莲叶南……"，指鱼儿只顾嬉戏于莲叶之间，而不贪饵上钩。"几许"和译文的疑问句型共同表达的是否定义。译文 East of the lotus leaves they swim 将"徒思"译成 they swim，将心理活动变成肢体活动，还原了诗人当时所见之景，也反映出原文重意象、译文重景象的特点。

6.2　归嵩山作

6.2.1　诗歌背景

开元中(713—741 年)，因为唐玄宗常住洛阳，所以王维从被贬官安置的济州(山东省济宁市)返回后，在靠近洛阳的嵩山也有隐居之所。在从长安(今陕西省西安市)回嵩山时，王维途中所见景色唤起了他安详闲适的心情，因此作此诗。《归嵩山作》描写了王维辞官归隐途中所见的景色，寓情于景，表达了诗人对辞官归隐的悠闲自得生活的向往。原文在句组间押尾韵，为 ABCB 结构，整首诗的译文是 ABAB 尾韵结构，体现了译者高超的用词和尾韵技巧。

6.2.2　古诗原文

归嵩山作

清川带长薄，
车马去闲闲。
流水如有意，
暮禽相与还。
荒城临古渡，
落日满秋山。
迢递嵩高下，

归来且闭关。

6.2.3　古诗译文

Back to Mt. Tower

The stream girdles the bog oblong;

My horse and cart move on, so free.

The gurgle loving flows along

While the homing birds chirp to me.

The bleak town near the ferry old

Sees fall peaks in the setting sun.

Mt. Tower looms far, rolling and rolled,

Now back home, I'm a lonely one.

（赵彦春　译）

◎ **注释**

1. Mt. Tower：located in the west of present-day Honan Province, one of the Five Mountains in Chinese culture. 嵩山

2. bog oblong：it refers to the swamp or marsh by riverside, covered with bush and trees. 长薄

3. bleak town：the town abandoned by residents for warfare. 荒城

4. looms far：it refers to the view of mountain from afar. 迢递

6.2.4　译文赏析

1. 清川带长薄，车马去闲闲。

译文：The stream girdles the bog oblong;

My horse and cart move on, so free.

赏析：原文在句组间押尾韵，为 ABCB 结构，整首诗的译文是 ABAB 尾韵结构，体现了译者高超的用词和尾韵技巧。"清川"指清清的流水与河川。"长薄"指草木交错丛生

的地方。"清川带长薄"意为清澈的河流沿着草木众生的地带流淌，其译文 The stream girdles the bog oblong 中，girdles 指紧紧缠绕，bog oblong 为椭圆形的沼泽，再现了原文的意象。oblong 为形容词后置，便于和下文的副词 along 形成尾韵。"闲闲"用重复的手法来强调悠然自得，而译文选择程度副词 so 来表强调，两者强调的目的一致，但方式各异。

2. **流水如有意，暮禽相与还。**

译文：The gurgle loving flows along；While the homing birds chirp to me.

原文："流水"的译文 The gurgle 指潺潺的流水声，用"流水"的声音来再现"流水"的形象。"如有意"指流水似乎对诗人充满情意，其译文为形容词 loving，置于 gurgle 后侧以体现文学风格。"暮禽"指傍晚的鸟儿，其译文 the homing birds 以归鸟的意象来对等原文的"暮"。译文 chirp to me 属于增译部分，对应上文的尾韵。由此可总结，译者形成尾韵常用的策略为形容词后置和增译。

3. **荒城临古渡，落日满秋山。**
   迢递嵩高下，归来且闭关。

译文：The bleak town near the ferry old，Sees fall peaks in the setting sun.
　　　　Mt. Tower looms far，rolling and rolled，Now back home，I'm a lonely one.

原文：译文的 ABAB 尾韵密度高于原文的 ABCB 尾韵。"荒城"在诗中指嵩山附近如登封等县城，史上屡有兴废，其译文 The bleak town 以阴冷来对等原文的荒凉。"古渡"指城池边古老的渡口，其译文 the ferry old 采用形容词后置策略，与下文的 rolled 形成尾韵。"迢递"指遥远的样子，其译文 looms far 指庞然大物隐隐约约地出现，而 rolling and rolled 体现的是山脉的起伏，属于为形成尾韵而增译的部分。

6.3　过太乙观贾生房

6.3.1　诗歌背景

"太乙观"原名万岁观，唐高宗时改为太乙观，并沿用至今，位于湖北省咸宁市龙潭乡蒋家洞村。"太乙观"因其传奇色彩、风景秀美和神奇的来历而备受游客青睐，每年的游客流量达 10 万余人。贾生曾与王维共同隐居终南山，那时他并未任职。《过太乙观贾生房》

描写了道观周围的风景、隐居的生活方式、道家对永生的追求和诗人对已故友人的思念。全诗的尾韵结构以 ABCB 为主，如邻、巾、春、臣、宾、新、真、人，译文与其一致。倒数第三、四句的译文最佳，皆为五言对偶句，为古诗翻译的一大至高境界。

6.3.2　古诗原文

过太乙观贾生房

昔余栖遁日，

之子烟霞邻。

共携松叶酒，

俱簑竹皮巾。

攀林遍岩洞，

采药无冬春。

谬以道门子，

征为骖御臣。

常恐丹液就，

先我紫阳宾。

天促万涂尽，

哀伤百虑新。

迹峻不容俗，

才多反累真。

泣对双泉水，

还山无主人。

6.3.3　古诗译文

A Visit to Sheng Chia's Room at Temple of the One

When I fled as a hermit then,

Amid mist and clouds you did dwell.

We did both carry pine-leaf wine,

An did both wear a bamboo shell.

We climbed and sought all crags and caves

And gathered wild herbs of all sort.

When I practiced the Word in the hills,

I was thought a page from the court.

I'd oft fear nectar was soon made

That earlier you'd join Purple Sun.

But you rushed to Hades too soon;

From all my pains grew a new one.

Solitude repels the vain world;

Learnedness may obstruct the true.

Now to the two fountains I cry;

Their host is gone, so much I rue.

（赵彦春 译）

◎ 注释

1. Sheng Chia: unidentified person, the poet's neighbor of seclusion. 贾生

2. the Word: referring to Tao if transliterated, the most significant and profoundest concept in Chinese philosophy. According to Laocius's *The Word and the World*: "The Word is void, but its use is infinite. O deep! It seems to be the root of all things." 道门子

3. Purple Sun: a renowned Wordist in the Tang Dynasty. 紫阳宾

4. Hades: the abode of the dead, and a euphemism for hell. 万涂尽

6.3.4 译文赏析

1. 过太乙观贾生房

译文：A Visit to Sheng Chia's Room at Temple of the One

赏析："太乙"古指太白山，为终南山的一部分，属秦岭山脉最高峰，为中华龙脉的一

部分。"观"指道观，因"太乙"又称太一，代表天地未分前的混沌之气，所以其译文为 Temple of the One。

2. 昔余栖遁日，之子烟霞邻。
　　共携松叶酒，俱篸竹皮巾。

译文：When I fled as a hermit then, Amid mist and clouds you did dwell.

　　　　We did both carry pine-leaf wine, An did both wear a bamboo shell.

赏析：译文的尾韵为 ABAB 结构，比原文的 ABCB 结构的尾韵密度大。"之子"指贾生，诗中被译为 you，代指标题所指之人。"烟霞邻"指隐居山中，以烟霞为邻，其译文 Amid mist and clouds you did dwell 采用的是过去时，以照应标题中的"过"字。"松叶酒"指用松叶煮水，加上适量的米酿成的酒，其译文 pine-leaf wine 用字面直译法，再现了源语字义，也直观地表达了饮品的原料。篸通"簪"，意为插或戴的动作。"竹皮巾"指一种用笋壳制成的帽子。为了与上句形成尾韵，译者将"竹皮巾"译成 bamboo shell，而非 bamboo hat。

3. 常恐丹液就，先我紫阳宾。
　　夭促万涂尽，哀伤百虑新。

译文：I'd oft fear nectar was soon made; That earlier you'd join Purple Sun.

　　　　But you rushed to Hades too soon; From all my pains grew a new one.

赏析：原文因"就"和"尽"的头韵，以及"宾"和"新"的尾韵，形成句子的 ABAB 结构，而译文为 ABCB 尾韵。"丹液"中的"丹"指丹药(也称九丹、还丹等)，"液"指金液，"丹液"为古代道士所炼的长生药，其译文 nectar 指甘露或植物中提取的琼浆玉液，在西方神话中喻意 the food and drink of the gods，与"丹液"意象一致。"紫阳宾"即紫阳真人，根据《云笈七签》卷一〇六《紫阳真人周君内传》："汉代周义山，入蒙山遇羡门子，得长生要诀，白日升天。"因"紫阳宾"为人名，属专有名词，所以其译文 Purple Sun 为大写，而译文的字面义也与"紫阳"一一对应，比拼音更利于外国读者理解。"夭促"指短命早死。"万涂尽"指人死后各种思绪终止。其译文 But you rushed to Hades too soon 中，But 译出了"夭促"的突发性，Hades 指西方地狱之神，too soon 表达了贾生在炼成升天仙丹前，突然死亡的遗憾。

4. 迹峻不容俗，才多反累真。

　　泣对双泉水，还山无主人。

译文：Solitude repels the vain world；Learnedness may obstruct the true.

　　　　Now to the two fountains I cry；Their host is gone，so much I rue.

赏析：原文因"俗"和"水"的尾韵，以及"真"和"人"的尾韵，形成 ABAB 结构，而译文为 ABCB 尾韵。"峻"指高峰，在诗中比喻归隐的生活，译文 solitude 将"峻"的喻义显性化。"累真"指有损人的真性和本性。译文 Learnedness may obstruct the true 中，Learnedness 通过动词的名词化和 the true 代指人的真性，来简化译文字数，将"迹峻不容俗，才多反累真"译文的字数控制为 5 个字，与原文字数完全对等，而字数的对偶与对等为古诗翻译的一大至高境界。

第三部分 赠答诗

第七章 深情慰问

7.1 奉寄韦太守陟

7.1.1 诗歌背景

公元 743 年，也就是唐玄宗天宝二年间，韦陟被李林甫排挤，官职从吏部侍郎贬为襄阳太守。王维对韦陟的遭遇深表同情，于是写了这首诗赠予他表示慰问，同时抒发自己内心的无限惆怅和悲凉。纵观全诗，首联概写孤城的萧条、荒凉，第二联描写肃杀的天气和哀鸣的孤雁，第三联从大景回归到细节，由远及近，层层递进。最后两联直抒胸臆，情感犹如开闸之水，奔涌出来，再也难以抑制。

7.1.2 古诗原文

奉寄韦太守陟

荒城自萧索，
万里山河空。
天高秋日迥，
嘹唳闻归鸿。
寒塘映衰草，
高馆落疏桐。
临此岁方晏，

顾景咏悲翁。

故人不可见，

寂寞平陵东。

7.1.3 古诗译文

To Prefect Chih Wei

The lonely town is cold and bleak；

The land looks void from rill to hill.

The sky's high，the autumn sun's far；

There linger wild geese trills so shrill.

The cold pondlet reflects grass dry；

To the house fall parasol leaves

It's time the year comes to an end；

Glancing back，I croon *Old Man Grieves*.

Your friend is not here，out of sight；

East of Level Wood you're in plight.

（赵彦春　译）

◎ **注释**

1. shrill：a shrill sound is high-pitched and unpleasant. 嘹唳

2. *Old Man Grieves*：the title of a verse in Chi Lu's prose *Percussion*，borrowed by the poet to express his loneliness. 悲翁

3. Level Wood：name of a wood on a level ground. 平陵

4. in plight：in a difficult or distressing situation that is full of problems. In the poem, Wei Wang conveys that Chih Wei was in trouble and he missed his friend very much. 寂寞

7.1.4 译文赏析

1. 荒城自萧索，万里山河空。

译文：The lonely town is cold and bleak；

The land looks void from rill to hill.

赏析：本句和下一句采用句尾押韵，"空"和"鸿"押韵，押/ong/。译文还原了句尾押韵，hill 和 shrill 押韵，押/ɪl/。这两句着重写景，有诸多意象。本句中"荒城"和"山河"，译者基本还原了原意象，分别译成 lonely town、hill、rill。其中 lonely town 中 lonely 一语双关，既描述出了边塞孤城地理位置偏僻，体现原文的"荒"，又可表达作者的孤独感，和诗歌最后两句的直抒胸臆形成呼应。void 在《柯林斯词典》中的解释为：You can describe a large or frightening space as a void. 该词用以表示"（空间）大而恐怖的"，突出河山空旷寂寥甚至有些阴森，间接译出了王维原作中的"空"，不仅是空间上的"空"，还是回首后，戍守边疆、保家卫国之事业付诸东流的"空"，今昔非比。

2. 天高秋日迥，嘹唳闻归鸿。

译文：The sky's high, the autumn sun's far;

There linger wild geese trills so shrill.

赏析：和上句一样，原诗句尾押韵，"空"和"鸿"押韵，押/ong/，译文还原了句尾押韵，hill 和 shrill 押韵，押/ɪl/。本句出现"天高""秋日"和"归鸿"的意象，译者基本还原了原意象，分别译成 The sky's high、autumn sun 和 wild geese。"迥"就是"远"，译者选择直译成 far，描述了秋日的高远。最后，译文中译者将"归鸿"稍作修改，译作 linger wild geese，linger 的意思是 continues to exist for a long time, often much longer than expected，突出了城外几点孤雁盘旋已久寻找同伴的悲戚，渲染了诗歌的意境，译者发挥主观能动性，使外国读者更加能体会到王维想表达的情感，可能诗人本身也就如同这归鸿，找不到同伴且身陷荒凉之地不能归乡。

3. 寒塘映衰草，高馆落疏桐。

临此岁方晏，顾景咏悲翁。

译文：The cold pondlet reflects grass dry; To the house fall parasol leaves.

It's time the year comes to an end; Glancing back, I croon *Old Man Grieves*.

赏析：第一句和下一句句尾押韵："桐"和"翁"，押/ong/，译者还原尾韵：leaves 和 Grieves。第一句译者直译出原诗所表达的意象和情景：寒冷的池水映照着衰败枯萎的草木，馆舍外那些梧桐也落了一地的叶子。第二句译者倾向于采用意译策略，译出原诗所表达的情感：又是一年结束的时候了，回首顾望吟咏《思悲翁》。

4. 故人不可见，寂寞平陵东。

译文：Your friend is not here, out of sight;

East of Level Wood you're in plight.

赏析：原诗不押韵，译者译出了诗歌的韵律，sight 和 plight 押韵，是译者主观能动性的体现。译者增加了两联的主语 you，增加了译文的可读性，同时通过用 is not here 和 out of sight 重复翻译"不可见"，以增加原诗表达的"不能见到朋友的悲凉感"。

7.2　寄荆州张丞相

7.2.1　诗歌背景

唐玄宗开元二十二年(公元 734 年)，张九龄为中书令，后提拔王维为右拾遗，在此之前王维只做过一些小官，在政坛上没有什么地位，所以王维视张九龄为伯乐甚至是恩人。此诗作于公元 737 年，当时张九龄被一个权贵集团迫害，被贬为荆州长史，举朝之士但求自保，无人敢说张九龄的好话，王维却不避权贵，特写此诗表达感念，当时王维还未真正归隐，充分体现出王维是一位知恩图报、不畏权贵之人。

7.2.2　古诗原文

寄荆州张丞相

所思竟何在，

怅望深荆门。

举世无相识，

终身思旧恩。

方将与农圃，

艺植老丘园。

目尽南飞雁，

何由寄一言？

7.2.3　古诗译文

To Premier Chang at Chaston

Where is the one whom I admire?

To Chaston I look and look higher.

None does me recognize on earth;

I keep in mind your grace and worth.

To the farmland there I will go;

Till old I will uphill crops grow.

I gaze at the south flying bird:

How can you send to him my word?

(赵彦春　译)

◎ **注释**

1. Premier Chang：Chiuling Chang（678 A. D. -740 A. D.），a famous premier and poet in the Tang Dynasty. 张丞相

2. Premier Chang at Chaston：Chiuling Chang was deposed to be secretary to the governor of Chaston. 荆州张丞相

3. Chaston：Chaste，Chingchow if transliterated，an old town on the Long River or a geographical region including areas of present-day Hupei and Hunan Provinces. 荆州

4. south flying bird：in the eyes of the ancients，the geese/bird always seem to be flying in the sky，just like people who are always on the road and displaced. Therefore，the imagery of south flying bird is associated with the sadness of travel and homesickness. 南飞雁

7.2.4　译文赏析

1. 所思竟何在，怅望深荆门。

译文：Where is the one whom I admire?

To Chaston I look and look higher.

赏析："思"本意是思念，译者意译成 admire，更加能体现出诗人在创作这首诗时对张丞相的情感，不仅有对张丞相的思念之情，还融合了三年前张丞相对自己的知遇之恩，《柯林斯词典》中对 admire 解释如下：You like and respect them very much or you look at them with pleasure. 充分体现了译者的主观能动性。

2. 举世无相识，终身思旧恩。

译文：None does me recognize on earth；

I keep in mind your grace and worth.

赏析：本句句尾和上一句的句尾处押尾韵，"门"和"恩"押/en/音，而译者选择在各个句子组内押尾韵，利于还原尾韵的修辞，也增加了译文的节奏和声调美，admire 和 higher 押/aɪə(r)/，earth 和 worth 押/ɜːθ/。译者用 recognize 对应"相识"，表达出王维诗中怀才不遇的困苦，直到他被张丞相赏识的情景。译者还将"思"和"终身"所表达出的意思理解并意译成 keep in mind，以还原原诗表达的对张丞相的知遇之恩于诗人来说是终生难忘的事实。同时增译 worth，既表达诗人对张丞相才华和价值的肯定，又完美形成尾韵，一举两得。

3. 方将与农圃，艺植老丘园。

译文：To the farmland there I will go；

Till old I will uphill crops grow.

赏析：同上句分析，译者译出句内尾韵：go 和 grow，同时增加头韵：To 和 Till，用另一种形式还原中国诗歌的节奏和声调美。译者根据上下文推测"谁"将与农圃，很显然定格为主人公王维在对恩公寄语，于是在译文中增加主语 I，符合逻辑，方便读者理解，也符合译入语特点。

4. 目尽南飞雁，何由寄一言？

译文：I gaze at the south flying bird：How can you send to him my word？

赏析：同理，译者根据上下文推测隐藏的代词，如"谁"将目尽南飞雁？何由"谁"寄一"谁的"言给"谁"？经分析，主角分别是 I、you、my 和 him，译文中进行了补充。"南飞雁"是本句的关键意象词，是中国古诗中常见的承载着独特文化内涵的意象，多表示羁旅情怀和思乡之情。译者采取直译的方法，其选词 south flying bird 与原作语言是对应的，保留了中国文化元素，而且字数对等。

7.3 酌酒与裴迪

7.3.1 诗歌背景

这是晚年的王维为劝慰友人裴迪而创作的一首拗体七律，作于其隐居辋川时期。裴迪因为遭受打击想不开，王维为了让好友好好吃饭、好好睡觉，专门写了这首诗，用愤慨之语对友人进行劝解，似道尽世间不平之意，也表现了王维欲用世而未能的愤激之情，在宽慰友人的同时也在宽慰自己，与好友一起用酒来浇化内心的忧愁。诗的首句说，斟酒与友人喝，劝慰他放宽心，人情往来反复，就像是波涛涌动似的一直都在。全诗风格清健，构思缜密。

7.3.2 古诗原文

酌酒与裴迪

酌酒与君君自宽，
人情翻覆似波澜。
白首相知犹按剑，
朱门先达笑弹冠。
草色全经细雨湿，
花枝欲动春风寒。
世事浮云何足问，
不如高卧且加餐。

7.3.3 古诗译文

Drinking with Ti P'ei

I pour you wine and you can feel at rest；

At changing feelings one may be distressed.

One still holds his sword on guard in old age;

Those advanced laugh at those new on the stage.

The greener grass has been moistened by rain;

When twigs sway, a cold wind will them restrain.

Worldly affairs are nasty things, ne'er mind;

We'd better eat more, reposed and reclined.

（赵彦春 译）

◎ 注释

1. holds his sword：it refers to an action of preparing to draw a sword to fight when angry. 按剑

2. Those advanced：according to historical records, Wang Ziyang became a high official in the Han Dynasty. Gongyu, his friend, was very happy when he heard of this. He brushed the dust off his hat and waited for his friend to promote him. Later, Wang Ziyang recommended him, but both were eventually dismissed. Wang Ziyang was the one advanced. The original intention is that the one advanced offer a helping hand, here the poet uses the opposite meaning, those advanced laugh at the later ones. 朱门先达

3. those new on the stage：as above, Gongyu is the one who was new on the stage. 弹冠

4. twigs：a twig is a very small thin branch that grows out from a main branch of a tree or bush. Here it means branches with flower buds. 花枝

7.3.4 译文赏析

1. 酌酒与君君自宽，人情翻覆似波澜。

译文： I pour you wine and you can feel at rest;

At changing feelings one may be distressed.

赏析： 原诗在整句话末尾押韵，比如本句的"澜"和后文的"冠""寒""餐"押/an/韵。虽然本句的两个短句未有尾韵，但译文增添了尾韵的修辞，还原了原诗的节奏美特点，如 rest 和 distressed 押韵。"自宽"表示自我安慰，译者采用意译手法译成 feel at rest，"翻覆"和"波澜"表达出诗人心中愤激之情，译者简单明了地用 changing feelings 代替，表达出人世间哪有什么真情，不过如波澜一样翻覆无常、时刻变化罢了，体现出译者对原诗的理解

之到位，译文降低了读者的理解难度。

2. 白首相知犹按剑，朱门先达笑弹冠。

译文： One still holds his sword on guard in old age；

Those advanced laugh at those new on the stage.

赏析： 原文虽无押韵修辞，但译文却增加了尾韵的特点，原文采用对仗修辞，译文采用尾韵修辞：age 和 stage 押韵，虽然形式不同，但都是诗歌的风格，译者译出了诗的风格。后半句的关键在"笑"字，译者对等译出动词短语 laugh at。本句有一个典故，弹冠即弹去帽子上的灰尘，据史书记载，汉代王子阳做了高官，他的好友贡禹听说后很高兴，掸去帽上的尘土，等着好友提拔自己。后来王子阳果然举荐他做了御史。"弹冠"本为援手荐引，乃同契之义，此处则反用其意，一旦"先达"（译成 Those advanced），即笑侮后来弹冠（出仕，译成 those new on the stage）者，轻薄排挤，乃至落井下石。译者对诗句进行了判断和理解，意译出诗歌所表达的典故用意，揭示了"朱门先达笑弹冠"的正确含义，说明这样的友情不可靠。

3. 草色全经细雨湿，花枝欲动春风寒。

译文： The greener grass has been moistened by rain；

When twigs sway, a cold wind will them restrain.

赏析： 本句写景，同上句一样，译文比原文多出了句组内尾韵的特征：rain 和 restrain 押韵。后半句正确的语序应该是 a cold wind will restrain them，译者通过改变译文的语序达成这个押韵，译成 a cold wind will them restrain。译文基本还原了原诗的意象，但是在"草色"一词中，译者发挥主观能动性，增加了比较级，增强了"青青春草，生机勃勃"和"也被雨全部打湿了"的强烈反差。

4. 世事浮云何足问，不如高卧且加餐。

译文： Worldly affairs are nasty things, ne'er mind；

We'd better eat more, reposed and reclined.

赏析： 同上句一样，译文比原文多出了句组内尾韵的特征：mind 和 reclined 押韵。同时 reposed 和 reclined 形成了诗歌的声乐重复，增强了诗歌的节奏美。诗人说"何足问"，也就是说不值得一提；浮云比喻世事犹如天上的浮云，不值得关心，这两者在原诗中其实是重复的，译者处理成 nasty things，直接表达出对世间万物的愤懑之情，突出了后半句所表达的"人生就应该吃得好睡得香"。

第八章 隐居志趣

8.1 辋川闲居赠裴秀才迪

8.1.1 诗歌背景

前面提到王维在辋川隐居时，和好友裴迪交往频繁。裴迪小王维十余岁，两人志趣相投，都有生活在终南山的经历，有过一段"浮舟往来，弹琴赋诗，啸咏终日"的美好时光。（《旧唐书·王维传》）该诗写于这期间，是他们互相酬赠的作品，也是王维的五律名篇之一。这首诗风光、人物交替行文，相映成趣，景与人融成了悠闲的秋日世界，抒发了闲居之乐和对友人的真切情谊。

8.1.2 古诗原文

辋川闲居赠裴秀才迪

寒山转苍翠，
秋水日潺湲。
倚杖柴门外，
临风听暮蝉。
渡头馀落日，
墟里上孤烟。

复值接舆醉，

狂歌五柳前。

8.1.3 古诗译文

To Showcharm P'ei from My Villa in Wangch'uan

The cold mountains deeper green grow;

The autumn rills more slowly flow.

By my door I lean on my cane;

Hearing cicadae sing their strain.

The ferry's touched with afterglow;

The village sees smoke upward go.

And I have seen Cart Joiner drunk;

Who, by Five Willows sing with spunk.

（赵彦春 译）

◎ **注释**

1. Showcharm：a talent recommended for official use or a well learned person in ancient China. A showcharm was usually well respected in the traditional Chinese society. 秀才

2. Cart Joiner：a hermit in Ch'u in the Spring and Autumn Period. A passage from Sir Lush reads like this：When Confucius went to the State of Ch'u, Cart Joiner, the mad hermit, came to his door："Phoenix, phoenix! Why is your virtue debased? The future we cannot see；the past we cannot catch hold of. When the world follows the Word, a sage completes all；when the world doesn't, he just survives. In this age, to stay free of penalty is the best. Good fortune like a feather is too thin to get；bad luck like the soil is too thick to avoid. Forget it, forget it! Do not show your virtue! Dangerous, dangerous! Scratch a path lest people go astray；brambles, brambles, do not creep and get in my way. O road, you bend and stretch away, do not bar my feet, o nay!"接舆

3. Five Willows：an allusion to Poolbright T'ao (352 A. D. -427 A. D.), a verse writer, poet, and litterateur in the Chin Dynasty. Pure and lofty, T'ao resigned from official life several

times to live a life of simplicity. There were five willow trees planted in front of his house, so he called himself Mr. Five Willows. 五柳

8.1.4　译文赏析

1. 寒山转苍翠，秋水日潺湲。

译文：The cold mountains deeper green grow;

The autumn rills more slowly flow.

赏析：译者将译文处理成句中押韵：grow 和 flow，原文"翠"和"湲"虽无押韵修辞，但译文却增加了尾韵的特点，翻译了诗的风格，而风格的表现方式是多样的。原诗两个较大的意象"寒山"和"秋水"，译者均还原出来，分别译成 cold mountains 和 autumn rills。原诗"转"是一个动词，在译文中译者巧妙运用意译策略帮助外国读者理解。转苍翠，表示山色愈来愈深、愈来愈浓，译者处理成比较级 deeper 表达出这个动态；cold mountains 是静止的，deeper 便凭借颜色的渐变而写出它的动态。同时 more slowly 和 deeper 形成形式上的对仗，也可以说是在句中尽量还原这首五言律诗风格对仗的特点，翻译出中国文化元素。

2. 倚杖柴门外，临风听暮蝉。

译文：By my door I lean on my cane;

Hearing cicadae sing their strain.

赏析：原诗的意思是"我拄着拐杖立在柴门外面，迎着风听秋蝉的叫声"，译者翻译的时候调整了顺序，运用倒装句，使得诗歌更加对仗，my cane 和 their strain 有一种朗朗上口的节奏美和韵律美。strain 的意思是 a state of worry and tension caused by a difficult situation，译者在译文中增加了拟人的修辞手法，将诗人的闲情和蝉的闲情融合在一起，更加凸显出诗人在隐居辋川时，过着十分安逸率性的生活。strain 的使用也增加了尾韵，一举两得。

3. 渡头余落日，墟里上孤烟。

译文：The ferry's touched with afterglow;

The village sees smoke upward go.

赏析：同上分析，上句末尾"湲"和本句的"烟"押/an/韵，但是原诗本句"日"和"烟"

并无押韵修辞，译文采用尾韵，afterglow 和 go 押韵，也算换了一种形式译出诗歌的特点。原诗对仗，把同类概念的"渡头"和"墟里"放在相对应的位置上使之出现相互映衬的状态，译者也将两个意象还原成 The ferry 和 The village，使译作保持原诗的韵味，同时句式结构也还原了对仗，译文都有主语、动词和介词。upward go 更是还原出"上"所表达的炊烟悠然上升的动态。

4. **复值接舆醉，狂歌五柳前。**

译文：And I have seen Cart Joiner drunk;

　　　　Who，by Five Willows sing with spunk.

赏析：同上分析，译者采用组内联句末尾押韵的手法，drunk 和 spunk 押韵，保留了古诗的音韵美。"复"的处理，译者没有采用直译策略译作 Again，这样处理恰到好处，因为原诗就不是表示又一次遇见裴迪，而是诗人情感的加倍和递进，表达王维"更遇良友"的快乐。在翻译过程中译者对原文的理解是非常重要的。

8.2　酬张少府

8.2.1　诗歌背景

此诗作于公元 741 年，是王维在半官半隐时期创作的。从题目上的"酬"看，张少府先有诗相赠，王维作诗解答。至于这位张少府对王维具体说了什么，我们无从得知，但是从全诗来看，大致可能是张少府问询"穷通"之理，劝诗人留心世务。开篇王维并没有直接回答问题，四句全是写情隐含着诗人晚年唯好清静的心态，颈联写的是诗人归隐"旧林"后的通达适意，尾联诗人借答张少府，用一问一答的形式，照应诗歌标题的"酬"。此诗反映了王维半官半隐时的精神状态，因为不想同流合污，只好走隐逸之路以求洁身自爱的心境。

8.2.2　古诗原文

酬张少府

晚年唯好静，

万事不关心。

自顾无长策，

空知返旧林。

松风吹解带，

山月照弹琴。

君问穷通理，

渔歌入浦深。

8.2.3 古诗译文

Thanks to Chang，a County Sheriff

In my late years I love quietude；

And about nothing do I care.

I think I have no good plan；

But retire to the old wood there.

The pine wind will untie my lash；

The hill moon will shine to my string.

If you ask me about the truth；

To the deep moor a song I'll sing.

（赵彦春　译）

◎ 注释

1. a County Sheriff：officer's title in the Tang Dynasty. 少府

2. the old wood：it refers to the former habitat of a bird. Here is a metaphor for the garden that used to live，Wei Wang's former residence. 旧林

3. The pine wind：an image in ancient Chinese poetry，representing nobility and purity. 松风

4. untie my lash：it refers loosely untie your clothes，indicates a state of leisure. 解带

8.2.4　译文赏析

1. 晚年唯好静，万事不关心。
自顾无长策，空知返旧林。

译文：In my late years I love quietude; And about nothing do I care.

I think I have no good plan; But retire to the old wood there.

赏析：原诗整体四个句子押尾韵，属于 ABCB 型，"心"和"林"均押/in/韵。原诗节奏清丽明快，一韵到底，流畅自如。译文同样还原了这种尾韵，本句的 care 和 there 押韵，充分做到与原诗形似。同时为了增加译文的可读性，译者增译了两句话中暗含的主语，从增加的 my 和 I 可以看出。后面不厌其烦地强调 I think、I have no 表达出王维的谦虚，增译 retire 突出王维人到晚年，政治思想和抱负幻灭，唯好清静的心态。

2. 松风吹解带，山月照弹琴。

译文：The pine wind will untie my lash;

The hill moon will shine to my string.

赏析："琴"与上文的"心"和"林"均押/in/韵，虽然最后一句末尾"深"并未押韵，但是译文增加了尾韵：string 和 sing 押韵，使得整首诗呈现联韵 ABCB 型，行文流畅。首先在前一句中"松风"和"山月"是中国古诗中非常重要的意象，均含有高洁之意。译者直译成 pine wind 和 hill moon，这种明显的异化手法保留了中文的名称和中国文化特色。同时，原诗用到了对偶的修辞。诗词中的对偶又叫做对仗。英文中没有对仗一说，译者处理成 "The+主语+will+动词/动词短语+my+宾语"的结构，亦是最大可能地还原出原诗的对仗美，后一句译者还原了原诗一问一答的形式。

3. 君问穷通理，渔歌入浦深。

译文：If you ask me about the truth;

To the deep moor a song I'll sing.

赏析：本句的 sing 和上一句的 string 押/iŋ/韵，还原诗歌的音韵美。"穷通"和"理"意思重复，"理"是"穷通"的上义词，为了实现译文的简洁流畅又保持原文意思不受影响，译者在翻译处理中保留"理"，译成 truth，将"穷通"省去不译了。同时，在"渔歌入浦深"中，译者增译出主语 I，帮助读者理解王维"世事如此，还问什么穷通之理，不如跟我一起归隐去吧！"的耐人寻味的诗中话。

8.3 答张五弟

8.3.1 诗歌背景

　　诗的题目是《答张五弟》，应该是张五弟有诗相赠，诗人为了回赠而写了此诗。张五弟，即张諲，唐代书画家，官至刑部员外郎，因排行第五，故称张五弟。王维中年以后在终南山隐居，和好友张諲情投意合。写此诗时王维仍在朝廷任职，但基本上处于半官半隐的状态，时常住在终南山中，在清寂的林泉中寻求精神寄托。这首小诗表现了诗人隐居终南山时寂静安闲的生活情趣，也表达了对志趣相投的友人的真挚感情。全诗风格亲切朴实，轻松自然。原诗整体六句中二、四、六偶行末尾"山""闲""还"同押/an/韵，译者在诗歌翻译中继承了将中国古典诗歌译为英文格律的经验，又有所改变，变成了每句句末押韵，如 I 和 eye、round 和 bound、fish 和 wish，增加了诗歌的节奏和声调美。

8.3.2 古诗原文

答张五弟

终南有茅屋，
前对终南山。
终年无客长闭关，
终日无心长自闲。
不妨饮酒复垂钓，
君但能来相往还。

8.3.3 古诗译文

My Answer to Brother Chang Fifth

In South End a thatched hut have I,

With the South Mountains eye to eye.

I have no guests, so it's closed all year round,

And all day I feel free, free without bound.

Why not have a drink or angle for fish?

You may come along or go as you wish.

（赵彦春 译）

◎ 注释

1. Brother Chang Fifth：Yin Zhang, Wei Wang's good friend who was a calligrapher and painter of the Tang Dynasty. He was also an official of the Ministry of Justice. He was called Brother Chang Fifth since he was the number 5 child in his family. 张五弟

2. South End：the southern urban area of Long Peace. 终南

3. the South Mountains：the Southern Mountains, also known as Mt. Great One, the mountains south of Long Peace, a great stronghold of the capital. 终南山

4. closed：here it means the poet closes the door to cut off outside contacts, not disturbed by the world. 闭关

8.3.4 译文赏析

1. 终南有茅屋，前对终南山。

译文：In South End a thatched hut have I,

With the South Mountains eye to eye.

赏析：译者在诗歌翻译中继承了将中国古典诗歌译为英文格律的经验，译诗句末押韵，本句的 I 和 eye 押/aɪ/韵。译者还原了意象"终南""茅屋""终南山"，在注释中第二点和第三点是译者做出的专有名词的解释，通过注解来解释诗歌中的地名的文化内涵，增加目标读者对诗歌内容和中华文化的理解。

2. 终年无客长闭关，终日无心长自闲。

译文：I have no guests, so it's closed all year round,

And all day I feel free, free without bound.

赏析：本句末的"闲"和上句末的"山"押/an/韵，译者还原诗歌音律节奏，本句两个

89

单词 round 和 bound 押韵。译者采用了英文中逻辑明晰的 so 结构，指明了"无客"和"闭关"的因果关系，因终年无客，所以门虽设而长关。译文还增补名词 bound，更加突出了诗人无拘无束、无忧无虑、无人打扰的隐居状态。此外，除了上文提到的译文的押韵处理，为了传达诗歌的节奏和声调美，译者在该句中还运用重复的手段，后半句重复了 free，译成 feel free，free without bound。

3. 不妨饮酒复垂钓，君但能来相往还。

译文：Why not have a drink or angle for fish?

You may come along or go as you wish.

赏析：原诗末尾"山""闲""还"同押/an/韵，本句句末押韵：fish 和 wish，译者译出诗歌体裁的风格，增加了诗歌的节奏和声调美。原诗采用白描手法，写自己饮酒、垂钓，都是赏心乐事。译者也采用直译的手法，还原"饮酒"(have a drink)、"垂钓"(angle for fish)，给读者展现了诗人隐居生活的情趣。前后两句的 or 增加了结构和节奏美感。

第九章 仕途之路

9.1 菩提寺禁裴迪来相看说逆贼等凝碧池上作音乐供奉人等举声便一时泪下私成口号诵示裴迪

9.1.1 诗歌背景

这首诗又称作《凝碧池》或《菩提寺禁裴迪》。唐玄宗天宝十四年(公元755年)十一月，安禄山造反。王维这一年转任给事中。公元756年，安禄山兵陷潼关，攻入长安，王维不幸被俘。当时王维被称为"天下文宗"，安禄山需要用他来装点门面。于是刀剑逼迫王维接受给事中职位，王维被迫接受伪职。这是诗人一生中最为伤心的经历，对诗人的后半生产生了重大影响。有一次，安禄山在凝碧池寻欢作乐，一位名为雷海青的宫廷乐师无法忍住内心的愤慨，在演奏中把乐器摔碎，向着唐玄宗的方向恸哭，结果被残忍杀害。裴迪把这个消息告诉了王维，王维听后感慨万千，挥笔写下这首诗回复裴迪。这首诗中，他的政治态度极其明确，倾述了国破之哀和思念朝廷之情。

9.1.2 古诗原文

菩提寺禁裴迪来相看说逆贼等凝碧池上作音乐供
奉人等举声便一时泪下私成口号诵示裴迪

万户伤心生野烟，
百僚何日再朝天。

91

秋槐叶落空宫里，

凝碧池头奏管弦。

9.1.3 古诗译文

I'm Jailed in Bodhi Temple and Ti P'ei Comes to See Me,
Telling of Lushan An's Party at Deepblue Pool for Musicians
While I Am Shaken to Tears with this Oral Impromptu to Ti P'ei

Ten thousand households mad with the wild haze,

When can my mates see the sky from the land?

To the vacant palace fall locust leaves,

While at Deepblue Pool there plays a string band.

（赵彦春 译）

◎ 注释

1. Bodhi Temple：when the An-Shi Rebellion broke out, Wei Wang was captured and imprisoned by Lushan An in the Boddhi Temple in Luoyang. The Bodhi Temple maybe is mistaken for the Pushi Temple, where Wei Wang was placed under house arrest in Luoyang, where there was only the Pushi Temple, and the Bodhi Temple was in Chang'an. 菩提寺

2. Deepblue Pool：a pool in Forbidden Park in Loshine, Tang's east capital. Lushan An occupied Long Peace and Loshine, the two capital of Tang, and he gathered a dozen officials and hundreds of musicians for a party to show his trophies. The musicians felt sad with tears in their eyes, and Lushan An would kill those who dared to cry. A musician called Sea Clear was dismembered at Horseplay Hall and was publicly exposed because he, flying into a rage, had thrown his instrument to the ground and cried to the west. 凝碧池

3. Musicians：Haiqing Lei（雷海青）, a famous musician who was good at playing the Pipa during the reign of Emperor Xuanzong of the Tang Dynasty. 供奉人

4. Ten thousand households：it refers to common people. 万户

9.1.4　译文赏析

1. **万户伤心生野烟，百僚何日再朝天。**

译文： Ten thousand households mad with the wild haze,

　　　　When can my mates see the sky from the land?

赏析： 原诗中的数词"万户"和"百僚"并非计数实指，是诗人常用以表达夸张的修辞，在这里表达出天下百姓亡国后悲痛不已。译者对"万户"进行直译，读者不会计较诗句的真伪，他们会从数字中真切感受到安史之乱后受到影响的人数之多。同时增加了 mad with，突出百姓的情绪是混乱的、失控的、疯癫的。对后者"百僚"，译者删除掉原诗的数词，意译成 my mates，主要受表达方式和篇幅的影响。

2. **秋槐叶落空宫里，凝碧池头奏管弦。**

译文： To the vacant palace fall locust leaves,

　　　　While at Deepblue Pool there plays a string band.

赏析： 汉语属于综合性语言，以意合方式成篇，古诗的内在逻辑比较模糊，需要读者深入理解。本句中译者增译 While，表达出上下两句之间的对比，帮助读者理解，使原诗的意思从模糊走向清晰：宫中空空如也，曾经的槐树叶子也凋零了，但是叛兵却在凝碧池寻欢作乐。"秋槐""空宫"是本句的重要意象，译者在译文中还原出来译成 fall locust 和 vacant palace，展现了诗人的悲，和后面形成鲜明对比。

9.2　献始兴公

9.2.1　诗歌背景

此首诗作于开元二十三年(公元735年)，是王维投赠给时任宰相张九龄的诗。开元二十二年(公元734年)，张九龄拜中书令，次年封始兴伯。张九龄很赏识诗人王维，在他任中书令的当年，提拔王维为右拾遗。本诗开篇表达诗人自己积极入世的态度，接着盛赞张九龄的开明，最后直抒胸臆："贱子跪自陈，可为帐下不?"希望自己在出仕拾遗后，能继续获得赏识和青睐。身为下属，王维写诗给上司，既表达了愿意有一番作为的求进之意，又表明自己不愿为了追求富贵而阿谀巴结王侯，写得不卑不亢。

9.2.2 古诗原文

献 始 兴 公

宁栖野树林，

宁饮涧水流。

不用坐梁肉，

崎岖见王侯。

鄙哉匹夫节，

布褐将白头。

任智诚则短，

守仁固其优。

侧闻大君子，

安问党与雠。

所不卖公器，

动为苍生谋。

贱子跪自陈：

可为帐下不？

感激有公议，

曲私非所求。

9.2.3 古诗译文

To Count of Rising

I would rather live in wild wood;

I would rather drink the creek flow.

I need not for dainties sit there

Or please lords and peers, bowing low.

A simple rural man I'd be;

In brown clothes till white hair I grow.

Wit and wisdom I fall short of;

To keep faith is what I can do.

I hear you are so fair and square;

With your sworn foe or bosom friend.

Public interests you do not sell;

To serve the masses is your end.

Now I fall on my knees to ask:

Can I give service in your tent?

I'll be gratified with your trust;

And do my best, not false or bent.

（赵彦春 译）

◎ 注释

1. Count of Rising: it refers to Jiuling Zhang, a famous Prime Minister in the reign of Emperor Xuanzong. 始兴公

2. dainties: it refers to the plural form of the word "dainty". We also could use "dainties of every kind" to express delicacy. 粱肉

3. brown clothes: it refers to commoners. A metaphor for a lowly person. 布褐

4. foe: Someone's foe is their enemy. 雠

9.2.4 译文赏析

1. 宁栖野树林，宁饮涧水流。

不用坐粱肉，崎岖见王侯。

译文：I would rather live in wild wood; I would rather drink the creek flow.

I need not for dainties sit there; Or please lords and peers, bowing low.

赏析：原诗采用对仗修辞手法，译文头两句还原了诗句的对仗，都采用"I would rather+动词"的结构，同时译文句尾押韵：flow 和 low，押/əʊ/音。"粱肉"指精美的膳食，形容富贵人家享用优渥，所以译为 dainties，译者选用 dainty（朗文词典中释意为：something small that is good to eat），突出了原诗表达的"精美膳食"的"精美"之意。would rather 和 need not 还原了"宁"与"不"一组词的对句，颇有力度。

2. 鄙哉匹夫节，布褐将白头。

译文：A simple rural man I'd be；

In brown clothes till white hair I grow.

赏析：译者基本还原了原意象，"匹夫"表示的是平民百姓，"布褐"指粗布衣服，借指平民，带有典型的汉语文化和思维特色。译者将前者意译成 simple rural man，译出原意象要表达的意思，后者直译成 brown clothes，与原作语言是对应的。

3. 侧闻大君子，安问党与雠。

译文：I hear you are so fair and square；

With your sworn foe or bosom friend.

赏析：大君子指张九龄，作者意译成 you，简单明了，但是原文中此词暗含敬意，诗人向所敬之人表达敬佩之意，所以译者增加了 so fair and square 来形容张九龄，以减少读者对诗歌的理解难度，表达作者听民间传颂张九龄身为一朝宰相，为官公正的内在含义。雠通"仇"，所以译成 foe。

4. 感激有公议，曲私非所求。

译文：I'll be gratified with your trust；

And do my best，not false or bent.

赏析：译文比原文多出了句组内尾韵的特征，如 tent 和 bent，押/ent/韵。上半句的"公议"表达诗人感慨世间有公正论，其实就是表达了作者感激张九龄的赏识和信任，所以译者进行意译，处理成 your trust，降低了读者的理解难度。同样地，下半句"曲私"表达诗人不求"偏私庇曲"，其实两者表达的意思差不多，而译文是 false or bent，译文和原文都用了词语重复策略，强调诗人尽管胸怀用世的强烈意愿，但绝没有借此谋求利禄的想法。

9.3 和贾舍人早朝大明宫之作

9.3.1 诗歌背景

这首七言律诗作于唐肃宗乾元元年(公元758年)春。贾至(718—772年),唐代文学家,曾任中书舍人。贾至曾写过一首《早朝大明宫呈两省僚友》,之后杜甫、岑参、王维都曾作诗相答,四人都在展现唐王朝的宫室之美、百官之富。本诗即为其中一首。这首诗按时间顺序,写出了早朝的全过程(早朝前的准备、早朝的威仪和早朝后的行动),既具艺术特色,写出了大明宫早朝时庄严华贵的气氛,又有史料价值。译诗整体增加了偶句尾韵 gown 和 crown、around 和 sound,译出了诗歌的音韵美和节奏美。

9.3.2 古诗原文

和贾舍人早朝大明宫之作

绛帻鸡人报晓筹,

尚衣方进翠云裘。

九天阊阖开宫殿,

万国衣冠拜冕旒。

日色才临仙掌动,

香烟欲傍衮龙浮。

朝罢须裁五色诏,

佩声归到凤池头。

9.3.3 古诗译文

In Reply to Secretary Chia's Poem:
the Levee at Great Bright Palace

The red-scarfed watchman heralds the new day;

The wardrobe keeper sends in His cloud gown.

The sky-high gates of the court open now;

Envoys from all kingdoms bow to the crown.

The plumed fans sway towards the morning sun;

Incense near His dragon robe wafts around.

Hued edicts you'll draft now ends the levee;

Phoenix Pool hears your pendants' clinking sound.

（赵彦春　译）

◎ 注释

1. Secretary Chia：referring to Chih Chia （718 A. D. -772 A. D.）, a poet and official who met Pai Li at Paridge after being degraded. 贾舍人

2. red-scarfed：it means wrap the head with red cloth like a cockscomb. 绛帻

3. watchman：in the ancient palace, when the sky was about to dawn, there were guards wearing red scarves who shouted loudly outside the Suzaku gate, like a rooster crowing. 鸡人

4. Phoenix Pool：alias of the Secretariat the poet Chih Chia chairs. 凤池

9.3.4　译文赏析

1. 绛帻鸡人报晓筹，尚衣方进翠云裘。

译文：The red-scarfed watchman heralds the new day;

　　　　The wardrobe keeper sends in His cloud gown.

赏析："绛帻""鸡人"和"晓筹"是典型的中国文化意象，"绛帻"表示用红布包头似鸡冠状。"鸡人"表示古代宫中天将亮时，有头戴红巾的卫士，于朱雀门外高声喊叫，好像鸡鸣，以警百官，故名鸡人。"晓筹"即更筹，夜间计时的竹签。译者注意到意象的传递，但是若直译成英文对读者来说也许有些陌生，这些意象词的内涵意义才是诗人需要表达的，译者再现原诗的情景，分别译成 red-scarfed、watchman 和 heralds the new day，英美读者凭借理解鉴赏力应该不难从中体会意象的含义及原诗的意境。"尚衣"是官名。隋唐有尚衣局，掌管皇帝的衣服。译者意译处理成 wardrobe keeper，直接将拥有该官名者的实际工作引入译诗，帮助读者理解。

2. 九天阊阖开宫殿，万国衣冠拜冕旒。

译文：The sky-high gates of the court open now;

Envoys from all kingdoms bow to the crown.

赏析：原诗"九天""万国"写出早朝的气势宏大，更能展现唐王朝的强大和威仪。"九""万"这两个数词不是真实的数字，诗中数词的运用主要是为了达到对比、夸张或其他修辞效果，译者分别处理成 sky-high gates 和 all kingdoms，还原了原诗夸张的修辞手法。

3. 朝罢须裁五色诏，佩声归到凤池头。

译文：Hued edicts you'll draft now ends the levee;

Phoenix Pool hears your pendants' clinking sound.

赏析：原诗没有主语，译者理解诗句之后在译文中增加了主语 you，译出了原文"早朝之后贾舍人就用五色纸起草诏书，那身上玉佩相撞的声音一直传到中书省"的情景。

第四部分 山水诗

第十章 野 游 登 览

10.1 终 南 山

10.1.1 诗歌背景

唐玄宗开元二十九年(741 年)至天宝三年(744 年),王维曾隐居于长安附近的终南山,此诗为隐居终南山期间所作。此诗又名《终南山行》或者《终山行》。诗人写了登山途中的感受以及途中遇见的风景,由远及近、由外入内、由低到高,从不同的视角,抓住不同的特征,用富有表现力的语言,渲染出终南山的神韵。首联写终南山的远景,"近天都"一词稍作夸张地渲染了终南山高耸入云、连绵不绝的浑茫气象。颔联由远及近,写登山途中的感受。颈联由高而下,写登上山巅的观感,突出终南山的辽阔幽深。尾联勾勒了一幅深山问路图,写出高山大壑带给人心的荒远幽深之意。原诗整体八个联句中二、四、六、八句偶行"隅、无、殊、夫"同韵,译者在诗歌翻译中继承了将中国古典诗歌译为英文格律的经验,又有所取舍改变,变成了句中押韵。

10.1.2 古诗原文

终 南 山

太乙近天都,

连山接海隅。

白云回望合,

青霭入看无。
分野中峰变，
阴晴众壑殊。
欲投人处宿，
隔水问樵夫。

10.1.3 古诗译文

The Southern Mountains

Great One does near Capital soar；
The ranges stretch onto the shore.
The white clouds behind merge as one；
The blue haze inside becomes none.
The main peak's a dividing line；
The dales are in shade or in shine.
Here I would put up for the night,
Asking a logger across：Right？

（赵彦春 译）

◎ 注释

1. The Southern Mountains：also known as Mt. Great One，the mountains south of Long Peace，a great stronghold of the capital. 终南山

2. Great One：Mt. Great One, i. e., The Southern Mountains；also a Wordist term, The One，indicating natural changes or the unification of everything. As *The Word and the World* says：The Word begets one，one begets two，two beget three，and three beget everything. 太乙

3. Capital：referring to Long Peace，the capital of Tang. 天都

4. the shore：The Southern Mountains does not reach the sea，which is an exaggeration. 海隅

10.1.4 译文赏析

1. **太乙近天都，连山接海隅**。

译文：Great One does near Capital soar；

The ranges stretch onto the shore.

赏析：译文句中押韵：soar 和 shore，原诗节奏鲜明欢快，译文亦是如此。"太乙"又作"太一"，指太一山，既是终南山的主峰，又是终南山的别称。近天都：犹言高与天连。天都，天帝所居之处，字面意思是天上的都市。"太乙"和"天都"都是明显具有中国文化特色的词语。译者将前者译成 Great One，首字母大写表达该词是专有名词——地名，带有一点归化倾向，表达出山的高大（great）形象，方便外国读者认识"太一山"在中国文化中的形象，同时"太一"和 Great One 形近且音近。而对于"天都"的翻译，译者处理成 Capital soar，soar 意为高飞，符合天帝之都的原意。原诗对仗，译文同样对仗，保留原诗特点。

2. 分野中峰变，阴晴众壑殊。

译文：The main peak's a dividing line；

The dales are in shade or in shine.

赏析："分野"是中国古天文学名词。古人将天上星宿和地上区域联系起来，把地上某一区域划在某一星空的范围之内，称为分野。中峰：指终南山的主峰太乙峰。此句意谓仅太乙主峰一山，已属于不同的分野，这就突出了终南山区的大。诗人用此来形容终南山的雄伟广大、气势磅礴。译者将"分"直译为 dividing（divide），"中峰"直译为 The main peak，由原诗可以看出，该句诗人描写的是峰顶的景色，视点是在山巅，"分野中峰变"描绘了"中峰"俊俏挺拔、直插云霄的雄伟之姿。直译出来让读者直观感受终南山的大和雄伟，有些文化负载词（如本句的"分野"）很难表达清楚，为避免画蛇添足，干脆直接表达原诗意思，使译文通俗易懂。

3. 欲投人处宿，隔水问樵夫。

译文：Here I would put up for the night，

Asking a logger across：Right？

赏析："欲投人处宿"这个句子省略了主语"我"，因而有此一句，便见得"我"在游山，处处有"我"，以"我"观物，译文处理得当，增加主语 I，更加符合英语语法规则。put up for the night 意为留宿，logger（lumberjack），《牛津词典》中意为（especially in the US and Canada）a person whose job is cutting down trees or cutting or transporting wood，此处译者采用归化手法，便于外国读者理解中国的樵夫形象。across 意为 from one side to the other side，表示樵夫在山涧的另一边。诗人既到"中峰"，则"隔水问樵夫"的"水"实际上是深沟大涧，很好地诠释出"隔水"之意，诗人侧首遥望的情景跃然纸上。

10.2　登河北城楼作

10.2.1　诗歌背景

　　此诗约作于唐玄宗开元十五年(727 年)，这个时候诗人已经隐居终南山，每天以山水为乐。一次，诗人登上附近的城楼，看到远处有山有水，近处人民安居乐业，心有所感，写下这首诗。诗人将村镇、客亭作一层远景；落日、苍山作一层中景；孤舟、渔家作一层近景，由远到近、由点到面再到点，构成了一幅层次错落、虚实结合、点面清晰的山川风景图。写景抒情，抒发了诗人内心自由快乐的情感和以山水为乐的情怀。

10.2.2　古诗原文

登河北城楼作

井邑傅岩上，

客亭云雾间。

高城眺落日，

极浦映苍山。

岸火孤舟宿，

渔家夕鸟还。

寂寥天地暮，

心与广川闲。

10.2.3　古诗译文

Composed on the Tower North of the River

A village abides Fu's Rock high;

A station dons haze from the sky.

The high town basks in the eve sun；

The water reflects the hill shone.

The lonely boat sways the bank fire；

The fishers with the birds retire.

The vast heaven and earth please me；

The broad river's calm and I'm free.

（赵彦春　译）

◎ **注释**

1. village：it refers to the houses and courtyards of the inhabitants，here the poet organizes it into "village". 井邑

2. Fu's Rock：the rock where Yueh Fu built a wall by stamping earth between board frames. Yueh Fu was a noble minister of high reputation in the Shang Dynasty. Historic records say that the King of Shang dreamed of a sage，and he sent people out to search for him and found Yueh Fu. 傅岩

3. the water：it refers to distant water surface. 极浦

4. the broad river：referring to the Yellow River. 广川

10.2.4　译文赏析

1. 井邑傅岩上，客亭云雾间。

译文：A village abides Fu's Rock high；

A station dons haze from the sky.

赏析：本句中原文有对偶修辞，译文虽然没有形式上对等修辞，但增加了尾韵的特点，high 和 sky 发音押韵，均发/aɪ/。诗人登上城楼看到村落，译文中的 high 体现出地理位置的高，译文直接传达出全诗布景在云雾之间。后半句译文采用拟人修辞，A station dons haze from the sky 的意思是"驿亭披上了烟雾一样的外衣"，形象生动地表现出原诗呈现的如梦如幻的迷离感。

2. 高城眺落日，极浦映苍山。

译文：The high town basks in the eve sun；

The water reflects the hill shone.

赏析：整首诗原文共四句，每一整句末尾字形成尾韵，本句的"山"和上一句末尾的"间"押韵，押/an/，译文则在 the eve sun 和 the hill shone 之间押韵，辅音/s/在分句中重复，读起来朗朗上口。"眺"意为"望，往远处看"，原文的主语也就是诗人被省略，译者没有直译为 look far，而是采用意译策略，译成 bask in，英文意思是 you lie somewhere sunny and enjoy the heat when you bask in the sunshine，直观表达诗人从高处仰望沉浸在落日美景中的情境，这正是原诗想要表达的意思。

3. 岸火孤舟宿，渔家夕鸟还。

译文：The lonely boat sways the bank fire；
　　　　The fishers with the birds retire.

赏析：原文分句组与上一句组形成尾韵，"还"的意思是"返还"，和上一句组结尾的"山"一样，发音均有尾韵/an/，而译者选择在句组内押尾韵：fire 和 retire；sways 生动形象地描绘出小船摇曳在水面上的画面，retire 的意思是 leave one's job and usually stop working completely，译文运用夸张的修辞手法，展现了渔夫生活的闲静，人民安居乐业，间接抒发出诗人内心的隐居之乐。

4. 寂寥天地暮，心与广川闲。

译文：The vast heaven and earth please me；
　　　　The broad river's calm and I'm free.

赏析：原文分句与上一句形成尾韵，"闲"同"还""山""间"押/an/韵。译者选择在句组内押尾韵：me 和 free，同押/iː/韵，译出了诗歌的节奏美。heaven and earth 的意思是天地间，译者增加了主语 me 和 I，强调出王维的心绪也跟那宽广的河水一般闲适，以帮助译者理解。

10.3　登裴秀才迪小台

10.3.1　诗歌背景

王维在辋川隐居时，和好友裴迪交往频繁。裴迪小王维十余岁，两人志趣相投并且都有生活在终南山的经历，有过一段"浮舟往来，弹琴赋诗，啸咏终日"的美好时光。(《旧唐书·王维传》)该诗写王维来拜访好友裴迪，恰巧好友不在，所以登上好友家的小台，登高眺望，于是记录下映入眼帘的满目云山——尽收于眼底的大自然之"绝景"，因而诗中之所写也就自然是对"绝景"的如实描绘或艺术再现。特别是第二联"落日鸟边下，秋原人外闲"十字所描绘之"绝景"，更是令人称绝。

10.3.2　古诗原文

登裴秀才迪小台

端居不出户，
满目望云山。
落日鸟边下，
秋原人外闲。
遥知远林际，
不见此檐间。
好客多乘月，
应门莫上关。

10.3.3　古诗译文

Climbing onto Showcharm P'ei's Platform

You need not go out of the door;
Clouded hills roll on to your eye.
All travelers gone, the plain is free;
Through afterglow, birds back home fly.
The distant wood I used to tour;
Now on your platform it's not far.
In moonlight I may oft come here,
Dear host, do leave your door ajar.

（赵彦春　译）

◎ 注释

1. showcharm：hsiuts'ai if transliterated，a talent recommended for official use through official examinations usually held every three years or a well learned person in ancient China. A showcharm was well respected in the traditional Chinese society. 秀才

2. clouded hills：the hills overcast with clouds. 云山

3. platform：it means Showcharm P'ei's platform. 檐间

4. ajar：if a door is ajar，it is slightly open. 莫上关

10.3.4 译文赏析

1. 登裴秀才迪小台

译文：Climbing onto Showcharm P'ei's Platform

赏析：诗的标题中的"秀才"是明显具有中国文化特色的词语，译者选用英文中和拼音"xiu cai"有相似发音的单词音译成 Showcharm/ʃəʊ tʃɑːm/，遵守了翻译的忠实性，既保留了中国文化特色，同时 charm 在《柯林斯词典》中的解释是：the quality of being pleasant or attractive(魅力)，让译文读者完全领略到中国特色文化的意趣，还能了解裴迪是一个令人欣赏的人，加上在后面进一步加注，解释何谓 showcharm，译者尽量还原和靠近"秀才"的本意，以帮助外国读者理解。

2. 端居不出户，满目望云山。

译文：You need not go out of the door；
　　　　Clouded hills roll on to your eye.

赏析：原诗虽没有主语，但表达的是裴迪闲居在家时不用出门，满眼就能望见云雾缭绕的山峰，译者采用增译策略，补充了主语 you 和 your，让诗歌更加符合英语语法规则，便于读者理解。"满目望云山"原本的主语是人，译者将主宾调换了顺序，同时动词 roll on 将 hills 拟人化，用夸张的手法突出裴迪家风景甚好，无需主人挪步，苍茫绵延的云山近在眼前的景象。

3. 落日鸟边下，秋原人外闲。

译文：All travelers gone，the plain is free；
　　　　Through afterglow，birds back home fly.

赏析：本句译者为了使二、四句末形成尾韵（eye 和 fly），将前后两联的顺序进行调换，充分地发挥了译者的主观能动性和对诗歌的二次创作力。"落日""归鸟"表达主人裴迪超凡脱俗、归隐的愿望；"秋原""人外"体现主人远离尘世的闲静。译者将这些意象基本上进行了还原（除了秋天这个时间因整体和谐做了省略处理）。译成 afterglow、birds back home、plain 和 travelers gone，增译 All（travelers gone），更加凸显出山林的寂静，进一步体现主人远离尘世，这种情感是和王维当下的心境高度契合的。

4. **遥知远林际，不见此檐间。**

译文：The distant wood I used to tour；

Now on your platform it's not far.

赏析：tour 和 far 共用尾韵/r/，译出了古诗的音韵美；相较于原诗，译者增译出主语 I 和 you，让句意更加完整，同时增加了两个时态，将过去和现在的情形作比较，表达出诗人闲来无事拜访，登高竟然无意间发现如此绝美的观景台的惊喜。

5. **好客多乘月，应门莫上关。**

译文：In moonlight I may oft come here；

Dear host, do leave your door ajar.

赏析：译文增加 dear（表明关系）和 do（进行强调），表达出作者和好友裴迪之间亲密无间的关系，也能让对这两位中国诗人不了解的外国读者更加熟悉裴迪的小台为什么可以得到诗人的认可和赞美，这是因为他们拥有同样的归隐之心，静心于山水之景。原诗整体八个联句中二、四、六、八句偶行"山、闲、间、关"同押/an/韵，译者在诗歌翻译中继承了将中国古典诗歌译为英文格律的经验，又有所取舍改变，变成了一五押韵：door 和 tour，二四押韵：eye 和 fly，六八押韵：far 和 ajar。

第十一章　潺潺流水

11.1　青　溪

11.1.1　诗歌背景

别名《过青溪水作》，是王维循青溪入黄花川游历的游记，大约是其初隐蓝田南山时所作的写景诗。诗的每一句都为一幅优美的画面，溪流随山势蜿蜒，百转千回，在乱石中奔腾喧嚣，在松林里静静流淌，水草随波浮动，芦苇倒映，在溪边的巨石上，垂钓老翁悠闲自在。诗句自然清淡，绘声绘色，静中有动，托物寄情，韵味无穷。其实，青溪并没有什么奇景，只有素淡的景致，为什么在诗人的眼中、笔下，会具有如此的魅力呢？就如王国维所说："一切景语皆情语也。"(《人间词话删稿》)王维以青溪之淡泊，喻自身之素愿安闲。

11.1.2　古诗原文

青　溪

言入黄花川，

每逐青溪水。

随山将万转，

趣途无百里。

声喧乱石中，

色静深松里。

漾漾泛菱荇，

澄澄映葭苇。

我心素已闲，

清川澹如此。

请留盘石上，

垂钓将已矣。

11.1.3　古诗译文

A Blue Stream

In the Yellow Flowers Stream I row,

Chasing blue ripples on the go.

Turning with the hills it does run,

For thirty miles, a trip of fun.

Against heaped rocks, it makes a noise;

Among deep pines, calm it enjoys.

The ripples push the water weed;

The pondlet mirrors the lush reed.

My simple heart is now at ease;

The blueness like this does me please.

Oh, on the boulder I would stay

And angle to finish my day!

(赵彦春　译)

◎ 注释

1. A Blue Stream：a stream in the east of Mianxian, Shaanxi. 青溪

2. the Yellow Flower Stream：a stream northeast of Phoenix County receiving water from Tasan

   Ridge, in today's Sha'anhsi Province. 黄花川

3. a trip of fun：it refers to the path travelled. 趣途

4. the lush reed：it floats over the blue stream, the reflection of the reeds reflected in the clear water. 葭苇

5. finish my day：I will live with it for the rest of my life. 将已矣

11.1.4　译文赏析

1. 言入黄花川，每逐青溪水。

译文：In the Yellow Flowers Stream I row,

　　　　Chasing blue ripples on the go.

赏析：原句没有主语，译者在翻译时增译了主语 I，交代了王维循青溪入黄花川的游历背景，增加了译文的可读性，便于理解；on the go 意为 busy，在译文中修饰 ripples(《柯林斯词典》：little waves on the surface of water caused by the wind or by something moving in or on the water)，译出了"溪水奔流不息，小浪花朵朵"的灵动感，译文不输原诗。我们都知道，"诗中有画"是王维诗的一大特色，他善于把握对象最鲜明的特征，展现其最引人入胜的一刹那，从而创造出山水写意画的艺术效果。译者尽量保留"诗中有画"的特点，忠实于原文的创造性，同时忠实于原文的意思。

2. 随山将万转，趣途无百里。

译文：Turning with the hills it does run,

　　　　For thirty miles, a trip of fun.

赏析：该句中的"转"和上句中第一行的"川"同押/uan/韵，译者在诗歌翻译中继承了将中国古典诗歌译为英文格律的经验，又有所取舍改变，变成了每一联都是句尾押韵：row 和 go，run 和 fun，读起来缓慢悠长、恰似水流。

3. 声喧乱石中，色静深松里。

译文：Against heaped rocks, it makes a noise；

　　　　Among deep pines, calm it enjoys.

赏析：原诗对仗，"里"和"中"是地理对仗，译文同样保持对仗，Against 对 Among，并且译文增加了尾韵：noise 和 enjoys，体现了中国古诗均衡美的特色；"乱石"译为 heaped rocks，heap 在《柯林斯词典》中意为 a pile of something, especially a pile arranged in

114

a rather messy way，忠实于原文，还原了该意象。同时为了便于读者欣赏，译者增加了两个主语 it，符合译入语的语法规则和行文特点。enjoys 是作者的增译，原诗句的目的是描述诗人心境的闲淡正如清川的闲淡，把自己的精神和自然的精神融合起来，意味隽永，这里的 enjoy 正有此意，运用拟人手法表达出深密的松林里悠闲自得的情绪，并且一语双关地表达出作者的内在想法，即享受当下的闲情逸致的状态。

4. *我心素已闲，清川澹如此*。

译文：My simple heart is now at ease;

The blueness like this does me please.

赏析：澹的本义是"水波摇动的样子"，也指恬静、安然的样子。原诗一语双关，既描绘出了青溪水波荡漾的景色，也有意将青溪作为自己的写照，以清川的淡泊、安然和恬静来印证自己的夙愿，译者选择译出后者的心境 does me please，实则是给前文这么多对青溪的描述予以总结，直抒胸臆地表达王维心中所念，毕竟译文中前几句多次出现 ripples，已经将这里想表达的澹的本义表达清晰，也避免了重复写景。does 进行了强调，和原文"如此"相对应。

11.2　汉江临泛

11.2.1　诗歌背景

唐玄宗开元二十八年(740 年)，时任殿中侍御史的王维，因公务去南方，途经襄阳。此诗是诗人在襄阳城欣赏汉江景色时所作的一首五言律诗，表达了其希望寄情山水、留恋山水的志趣和追求美好的思想感情，也隐含了歌颂地方行政长官的功绩之意。首联写众水汇聚，为整个画面渲染了气氛；颔联写江水浩荡、一泻千里，流出人们的视野，"江流天地外，山色有无中"历来为人们所传诵，不愧为千古佳句；颈联写出眼前波澜壮阔之景，渲染了磅礴水势；尾联直抒胸臆。本诗从线条、色彩、构图诸方面具体体现了王维后期诗歌中的水墨山水意境，表现出诗人融画入诗的高超才能。

11.2.2　古诗原文

汉江临泛

楚塞三湘接，

荆门九派通。

江流天地外，

山色有无中。

郡邑浮前浦，

波澜动远空。

襄阳好风日，

留醉与山翁。

11.2.3 古诗译文

Boating on the River Han

It flows back to Three Hsiangs from Ch'u;

And through Chastegate to the Nine blue.

The waters outrun earth and sky;

The misty hills heave low or high.

The town ashore seems there to drown;

The dome shakes as if to fall down.

O Sowshine's good sights do please me;

I will drink with Hillman, care-free.

（赵彦春 译）

◎ 注释

1. the River Han：the Han River, the longest branch of the Long River, having an important position in Chinese history. 汉江

2. Three Hsiangs：referring to present-day Hunan Province. The Hsiang River flows into three rivers, the Li, the Cheng and the Hsiao, hence the name Three Hsiangs. 三湘

3. Ch'u：a vassal state of Chough, one of the powers in the Warring States Period, conquered and annexed by Ch'in in 223 B. C. 楚塞

4. Chastegate：Chingmen if transliterated, an important city in today's Hupei Province. 荆门

5. the Nine blue：the Nine Rivers, that is, Bankshine, today's Chiuchiang, Chianghsi

Province or the nine rivers in this area, after which the city was named. 九派(指长江的九条支流,长江至浔阳分为九支。相传大禹治水,开凿江流,使九派相通。)

6. Sowshine：a famous historic city, about 2,800 years old, a birthplace of Ch'u, Han and Three Kingdom cultures, and a city of economic and military importance, in the northwest of present-day Hupei Province. 襄阳

7. Hillman：referring to the fifth son of Shan Tao, one of the Seven Sages of the Bamboo Grove in the Chin Dynasty. He was as gentle and graceful as his father. When he was an official, the nation was falling apart and other officials were worried and depressed. Hillman, however, lived a casual life. When he hanged out, he used to hold a banquet and get drunk at the High Sun Pool. 山翁

11.2.4 译文赏析

1. 楚塞三湘接,荆门九派通。

译文：It flows back to Three Hsiangs from Ch'u;

And through Chastegate to the Nine blue.

赏析："楚塞""三湘""荆门"和"九派"都是明显具有中国文化特色的词语,作者音译成 Ch'u、Three Hsiangs、Chastegate(Chingmen)和 the Nine blue 并且加以解析,遵守了翻译的忠实性,保留了中国文化特色和原诗的古意,让译文读者完全领略到中国特色文化的意趣。

2. 江流天地外,山色有无中。

译文：The waters outrun earth and sky;

The misty hills heave low or high.

赏析：原诗分句末押韵,译文则采用组内分句末尾押韵的手法,如本句的 sky 和 high,译出诗歌的韵律,且 earth and sky 和 low or high 形式上对仗,保留了原诗均衡美的特色。"江流"译成 waters,给人一种水漫天地之间的直观感,写出江水的流长邈远;后半句 misty 的山景迷迷蒙蒙、时隐时现、若有若无,忠实于原文的"有无中",low or high 体现出两岸重重青山高低不一的状态;heave 在《柯林斯词典》中的解释为 If something heaves, it moves up and down with large regular movements,给读者非常强烈的画面感。此句组的译文描写了苍茫山色和层峦叠嶂的山景与江水融为一体的壮观画面,给予读者强烈

117

的画面感。

3. 郡邑浮前浦，波澜动远空。

译文： The town ashore seems there to drown；

The dome shakes as if to fall down.

赏析： 原诗运用对偶修辞，并且本句的"空"和前面诗句末尾的"通""中"押/ong/韵，译者在翻译时刻意将本句句末押韵：drown 和 down，营造一种波涛的汹涌澎湃之感，对烘托诗意起到很大作用。同时译文 The town ashore 和 The dome shakes 也有对偶的效果，seems 和 as if 意思相同，译者尽量还原诗歌的修辞手法。

4. 襄阳好风日，留醉与山翁。

译文： O Sowshine's good sights do please me；

I will drink with Hillman，care-free.

赏析： 同上句，译者采用组内分句末尾押韵的手法，me 和 care-free 押韵，保留了古诗的音韵美；译者采用直译和增译的方式翻译出原诗，增译了 do please me，直抒胸臆，表达出"好风光"给诗人以美的享受，并增译 care-free（don't have or involve any problems，worries，or responsibilities），表达诗人想留下和山翁醉饮千盅、留恋山水的志趣，这正是原诗想传达的情感，译文虽然没有忠实于原文形式，但是忠实于原文所表达的意思。

11.3　鸟　鸣　涧

11.3.1　诗歌背景

《鸟鸣涧》是王维写景诗的代表作之一，为王维青年时期游历江南之时所作。作于开元（唐玄宗年号，713—741 年）年间，其背景是安定统一的盛唐社会。此诗是组诗《皇甫岳云溪杂题五首》的第一首，是诗人寓居在今绍兴县东南五云溪（即若耶溪）的作品。诗中描绘了一幅春夜溪涧人迹稀少、桂花飘落、夜静月出、空山鸟语的唯美图景，全诗紧扣一个"静"字，但是"花落""月出""惊山鸟""时鸣"等词又是动景，以动衬静，侧面表达了盛唐时期和平安定的社会氛围。

11.3.2　古诗原文

鸟 鸣 涧

人闲桂花落，
夜静春山空。
月出惊山鸟，
时鸣春涧中。

11.3.3　古诗译文

Birds Twitter o'er the Brook

I idle cassia flowers to fall；
Night quiets the vernal hills o'er all.
The moon out，startled birds flutter；
At times，o'er the brook they twitter.

（赵彦春　译）

◎ 注释

1. Brook：a brook is a small stream. 涧

2. Birds Twitter o'er the Brook：as its name implies，it is a mountain stream with birds singing.
   鸟鸣涧

3. idle：idle is used to describe something that you do for no particular reason，often because
   you have nothing better to do. 闲

4. o'er：o'er means the same as "over". 中

11.3.4　译文赏析

1. 鸟鸣涧

译文：Birds Twitter o'er the Brook

赏析：译者采取直译策略，和原诗标题"鸟鸣涧"对等，忠实地再现了原诗的意义。

2. 人闲桂花落，夜静春山空。

译文：I idle cassia flowers to fall;

Night quiets the vernal hills o'er all.

赏析：原诗运用对偶修辞，并且原诗的"空"和第四行末尾的"中"押/ong/韵，营造了一种深山古刹的悠远钟声久久回荡的效果，从而使山谷显得更加空旷寂寥，对烘托诗意起到很大作用。译者虽没有追求翻译形式上的对等，但采用句组内尾韵的手法，如 fall 和 all，同样可以营造相似的效果，/ong/韵和/ɔːl/发音非常相似，凸显山谷的空旷和寂寥。同时译者从直译层面将隐含的"我"翻译出来。

3. 月出惊山鸟，时鸣春涧中。

译文：The moon out, startled birds flutter;

At times, o'er the brook they twitter.

赏析：译文同样采用句组内尾韵的手法，如 flutter 和 twitter，使得诗歌读起来朗朗上口，也同样能达到原诗对偶修辞赋予诗歌本身的效果，韵律和谐，节奏感强。另外，王维创造这首诗时身处盛唐，诗中的意象"月出""鸟惊""时鸣"等组成的是一幅兴兴向荣、祥和的画面，折射出盛唐和平安定的社会氛围。因此"鸣"均译作 twitter(When birds twitter, they make a lot of short high-pitched sounds)非常贴切，表达鸟儿叽叽喳喳欢快地叫。startle (it surprises and frightens you slightly)意思是轻微受惊吓，在意境的烘托方面多了一丝活力，描绘了一幅动静结合的画面。

第十二章　辋川胜景

12.1　鹿　柴

12.1.1　诗歌背景

唐玄宗天宝年间，王维在终南山下购置辋川别业。鹿柴是王维在辋川别业的胜景之一。辋川有胜景二十处，王维和他的好友裴迪逐处作诗，编为《辋川集》，共二十首，《鹿柴》是其中的第五首。本诗描写了傍晚时分的景象：落日夕阳，空山无人，此时光线透过茂密的树林照射到林地的青苔上，顿时冷寂的山林有了一丝光亮，诗人捕捉到了余晖照到青苔上一闪而过的情景，把禅意渗透于自然景色的生动描绘之中，创造了一个空寂幽深的境界：山中空旷寂静看不见人，只听得说话的人语声响；夕阳的金光直射入深林，又照在幽暗处的青苔上。该诗语言清新自然，以动衬静，表现了作者在深幽的修禅过程中的豁然开朗。

12.1.2　古诗原文

鹿　柴

空山不见人，

但闻人语响。

返景入深林，

复照青苔上。

12.1.3 古诗译文

The Deer Fence

In the mountains no one is found;

But his voice is heard to resound.

The deep wood sees the returned sun;

Once again the green moss is shone.

（赵彦春 译）

◎ **注释**

1. The Deer Fence：probably a pen where deer are kept in a hill wood. 鹿柴

2. But：only，here it means that only his voice is heard. 但

3. the returned sun：sunlight reflected by clouds when the sun is going down. 返景（ying），同"影"

4. … is shone：shone is the past tense and past participle of shine，referring to a buddhist term which is a figurative expression of Zen enlightenment（禅宗）. 复照

12.1.4 译文赏析

1. 空山不见人，但闻人语响。

译文：In the mountains no one is found;

But his voice is heard to resound.

赏析：原诗分句末押韵，译文则采用组内分句末尾押韵的手法，如本句的 found 和 resound，译出诗歌的韵律；"空山"和"不见人"意境重合，译者为避免累赘，只译出了 no one，就表明了"空山"，实在是妙；对于"人语响"的翻译，译文 his voice is heard to resound 较符合诗歌的情境，resound 在《柯林斯词典》中的解释是 If a place resounds with or to particular noises, it is filled with them，体现出人语应该是在空旷的深林中回荡不息的特点，再现原诗的内涵；同时，"不见人"与"但闻人"，"人"字是重复的。译文中以 no one/

his 相对应，不费力地保留了原诗的对仗，采用同样的译法保留诗歌对仗结构的还有两个被动语态 is found 和 is heard。

2. 返景入深林，复照青苔上。

译文：The deep wood sees the returned sun;

Once again the green moss is shone.

赏析：原文分句组末尾与上组末尾押韵，如本句的"上"和上一句的"响"，都是/ang/音，而译文则采用组内分句末尾押韵的手法，如 sun 和 shone；"深林"译为 deep wood，给人山林茂密的感觉。"复照"并非是"反射而照"，因此译文 green moss is shone 比较贴切，再现了夕阳斜照落到青苔上的瞬间景象，此时的诗人灵光一闪，顿时醍醐灌顶，在瞬间顿悟，思想到达了永恒的境界。

12.2　栾　家　濑

12.2.1　诗歌背景

王维隐居在辋川的时候，既不用操心朝廷事务，也不用亲自耕种，每日所做的事情就是在辋川附近游历山水，或与朋友一同游历或独行其乐，此时的诗人非常之闲适，这种理想境界正是刚走出政治旋涡的诗人所追求的。辋川有胜景二十处，该诗是《辋川集》诗二十首之第十二首。全诗短短四句，前两句营造了一幅闲适的画卷：在秋雨的沙沙声中，伴随着石头上的水流哗哗作响；后两句写溪流相互碰撞，受了惊的白鹭飞起又落下。整首诗毫无华丽字眼，但是每一句景物描写都弥漫着一种淡雅之气，读来韵味深长。宋代刘辰翁在《王孟诗评》中对该诗有着高度评价："此景常有，人多不观，唯幽人识得。"

12.2.2　古诗原文

栾　家　濑

飒飒秋雨中，

浅浅石溜泻。

跳波自相溅，

白鹭惊复下。

12.2.3 古诗译文

The Gushing Rapids

Soughing, soughing, the autumn rain,

Shallow, shallow, the brook on stone.

The waves run with a splashing tone;

The egret shocked alights again.

（赵彦春 译）

◎ **注释**

1. The Gushing Rapids：a section of rapids of the Wangch'uan River originating from Mt. Wangch'uan. 栾家濑

2. soughing：the sound of wind and rain；（esp. of the wind）to make a characteristic sighing sound. 飒飒

3. shallow：the sound of rushing water. 浅浅

4. the brook：it refers to the rushing water over rocks. 石溜

12.2.4 译文赏析

1. 飒飒秋雨中，浅浅石溜泻。

译文：Soughing, soughing, the autumn rain；

Shallow, shallow, the brook on stone.

赏析：原诗不押韵，译文押 ABBA 韵。如本句中的 rain 和第 4 句末尾的 again 押尾韵 /eɪn/，形成诗歌的音韵美。原文中此分句组采用了重复的手法，重复了"飒"和"浅"字，"飒飒"表现风雨之声，与之对应的叠字"浅浅"表现溪水的湍急，极具音乐美。译文的这两句同样采用重复的手法，重复了"soughing"和"shallow"两个词汇，不仅塑造出了可感的画面，也让读者体会到溪水流动的潺潺之声，画中见声。译者在翻译诗歌的时候，由于文本体裁的特殊性，不仅要忠实于原文的意思，如果可以，做到忠实于原文格式是非常难能可贵的；并且译者通过使用"Soughing，soughing"和"Shallow，shallow"两个押头韵/s/的词汇，描绘"在秋雨的沙沙声中，那浅浅的溪水跳过石头轻快地流动"的情景，使画面显得和谐统一的同时，译文也和谐统一。

2. 跳波自相溅，白鹭惊复下。

译文：The waves run with a splashing tone；

The egret shocked alights again.

赏析：原诗不押韵，译文押 ABBA 韵。如本句中的 tone 和译文第 2 句末尾的 stone 押尾韵/təʊn/，形成诗歌的音韵美。本句两联诗人运用动静结合的手法，写出了水珠飞溅，惊起了觅食的白鹭，待白鹭得知为虚惊后又飞回原处的安静祥和的画面。译者用 run 和 a splashing tone 不仅将溪水拟人化，更将欢快流动表达得淋漓尽致。"白鹭惊复下"中的"惊"本是白鹭受到惊吓，译者将动词处理成后置定语修饰白鹭，简单明了又不失原诗意思，极具画面感。

12.3 辛 夷 坞

12.3.1 诗歌背景

自唐玄宗开元二十四年(公元 736 年)当朝宰相张九龄被罢免，李林甫一派势力上台，朝政黑暗，社会矛盾日趋尖锐。王维倾向于张九龄的开明政治，且张九龄非常赏识王维，王维对现实十分不满而又无能为力，产生退隐归田的思想而又恋于禄位，思想矛盾。于是在长安附近的终南山下辋川建立别墅，过着亦仕亦隐的生活。该诗是《辋川集》诗二十首之第十八首，全诗短短四句，诗的前两句着重写花的"发"。当春天来到人间，辛夷欣欣然地绽开神秘的蓓蕾，绚烂夺目，好似云蒸霞蔚，显示着一派春光。诗的后两句写花的"落"，它自开自败，顺应着自然的本性，它自满自足，无人欣赏，也不企求有人欣赏。王维将禅境的内心与幽寂的自然景物结合，描绘了辛夷花的美好形象的同时，又写出了一种落寞的景况和环境。

12.3.2 古诗原文

辛夷坞

木末芙蓉花，
山中发红萼。
涧户寂无人，
纷纷开且落。

12.3.3 古诗译文

A Lily Magnolia Grove

Like lotus buds red on sprays,
Uphill lily magnolias flower.
By the creek there's no human trace,
But blossoms burst and petals shower.

（赵彦春 译）

◎ 注释

1. lily magnolia：also known as magnolia wood with blooms looking like lotus flowers，pink，purple or white. 辛夷

2. uphill：near the top of a hill or are going up a slope，is also an adjective. 山中

3. creek：a creek is a small stream or river. 涧

4. petals shower：here it refers to the situation when a lot of petals fell，the same as the rain. 开且落

12.3.4 译文赏析

1. 木末芙蓉花，山中发红萼。

译文：Like lotus buds red on sprays,

Uphill lily magnolias flower.

赏析：王维原诗中，景色与内心的禅意融为一体，诗人以"木末""山中""涧户"等意象营造出一种静寂空灵的意境，译者在翻译过程中，极大地还原了这种意境。译文中的 lotus buds、uphill、lily magnolias 和 flower 完整地还原了原诗的意象，在英文语言中利用原本的意象重新构建了原诗的意境，直译出意象并且罗列出来，看似简单，实则搭建了一种"空灵"的意境；翻译过程中融入了译者的想象与主观能动性，实现了该句在英译过程中意境特征的审美再现。同时还原诗的动静结合，本句描述的是静态的辛夷花的翻译处理。静态辛夷花状态的翻译用了 on 这个介词，表示状态是"枝头上的"，其次抓住了辛夷花"发"这一动作，将其翻译成 uphill（《柯林斯词典》解释：If something or someone is uphill or is moving uphill, they are going up a slope），表达出辛夷花发出枝头的动作，实现了动静结合特征的再现。

2. 涧户寂无人，纷纷开且落。

译文：By the creek there's no human trace,

But blossoms burst and petals shower.

赏析：前半句"无人"意译成 no human trace 而不是直接译成 no one，较好地体现出原诗的"寂"，保留了原诗落寞的景况和环境。原诗后半句写花的"落"，它自开自败，顺应着自然的本性，是动态中的辛夷花。译者的翻译处理也保留了"动"，并列使用 burst 和 shower，将辛夷花动态的开落过程完美地呈现出来，同时充分发挥了译者的主观能动性，增加了主语 blossoms 和 petals，画面感十足。同时表现出时间的流逝之感，blossoms 最终变成了 petals 凋零，生动形象地译出了花苞绽放和花瓣凋零的全过程，既有创造又保留了原诗的意境。

第五部分 咏物诗

第十三章 抒发情怀

13.1 相　　思

13.1.1 诗歌背景

《相思》是借咏物而寄相思的诗歌。红豆，又名相思子，人们都将它看作爱情的象征。诗人咏此物以寄相思，已不是在追述那位树下思念丈夫的妻子肝肠寸断的故事，亦可包括友情，境界更高了。红豆，生于南方，诗歌写相思之情，却全篇不离红豆。全诗情调高雅，怀思饱满奔放，语言朴素无华，韵律和谐柔美。据说，天宝之乱后，著名歌者李龟年流落江南，经常演唱它，听者无不动容。

13.1.2 古诗原文

相　　思

红豆生南国，
春来发几枝。
愿君多采撷，
此物最相思。

13.1.3 古诗译文

The Love Bean

The red bean grows in Southern Land.

How many twigs shoot forth in spring?

Pray pick, pick more to fill your hand;

To speak for love, 'tis the best thing.

（赵彦春 译）

◎ 注释

1. the red bean：a kind of red seed produced by ormosia in tropical and subtropical southern areas, a symbol of love. 红豆

2. Southern Land：a city in Nanchong, Sichuang Province. 南国

3. twig：a slender shoot of a tree or other plant. 枝

4. shoot forth：the part grows up from the ground when a plant starts to grow；a new part of plants or trees grows. 发

13.1.4 译文赏析

1. 红豆生南国，春来发几枝。

译文：The red bean grows in Southern Land.

How many twigs shoot forth in spring?

赏析：本首诗采用一般现在时态，更能使诗行呈现不拘于时空的朦胧美。在语态使用上，采用主动语态，强调了"红豆"生长在南国这一自然现象，和原文更加接近。为了表达刻骨的相思，只用了一个"红"字，就把炽热的情思充分流露出来，译者也将其译为 red bean，使得译文更加接近原文。"南国"表地点，译为 Southern Land，忠实地传达了原诗的信息。"春来发几枝"为肯定句，译者将其译为疑问句，设问非常自然，与听众的距离也因此拉近。"春来"把"来"这个动词进行了词性转换，作为副词表时间，处理为 in spring。原诗二、四句"枝""思"押/i/韵，全诗尾韵为 ABCB 模式，译文采用 land 和 hand、spring 和 thing 押韵，即 ABAB 的押韵模式，也充分体现了诗歌的音美。另外，译者注重了译文结构的工整对仗，一、二句七个音节，读起来朗朗上口，节奏感强，完美再现了原诗的节奏之美。

2. 愿君多采撷，此物最相思。

译文：Pray pick, pick more to fill your hand；

To speak for love, 'tis the best thing.

赏析：《相思》是一首五言绝句，格律严谨优美，译者采用了长句变为短句的译法，将"愿君多采撷"分成两个小句，即"愿君采，愿君多采"（pray pick, pick more...），而这种方式，也就是连续重复，增加了诗歌的情感，也使得句子更加流畅、朗朗上口。为了形成对照，"此物最相思"也处理为两个句子，即 To speak for love 和 'tis the best thing。所以，三、四句共八个音节，长度相等，译文和原文形似，对仗工整，这种工整的对仗使译文读起来朗朗上口。

13.2 红 牡 丹

13.2.1 诗歌背景

本首诗展现出牡丹花开花落，不受人事活动和心情的干扰，自然开放，即景会心，被诗人的瞬间直觉捕捉住，自然灵妙地描绘出来。体现了王维意境之创造和抒情之追求，皆是与自然的认知息息相关的。诗人以自然景物为材料，通过直觉引发意象，从而诗歌具有天然风神，又避免过分雕琢之感，达到真朴自然、抒发真情、绘景逼真、自在风流的特色。诗人通过描写牡丹来感慨时光。这首诗前两句写牡丹娇艳可爱的丰姿和闲雅安静的气度，后两句写红牡丹花心之愁及不被春色所知的怅惘，诗人赋予红牡丹以人的悲戚形态，含蓄蕴藉，余味悠长。

13.2.2 古诗原文

红 牡 丹

绿艳闲且静，
红衣浅复深。
花心愁欲断，
春色岂知心。

13.2.3 古诗译文

The Red Peony

Her green leaves stay free and serene;

Her red blouse does glisten and sheen.

The sadness cuts her through, so smart;

Do the hues of spring know her heart?

（赵彦春　译）

◎ 注释

1. peony：a symbol of fecundity and dignity in Chinese culture, esteemed as the king of flowers. 牡丹

2. serene：calm, peaceful, or tranquil; unruffled. 静

3. glisten：to reflect a sparkling light or a faint intermittent glow; shine lustrously. 浅

4. sheen：luster; brightness; radiance. 深

5. hue：a gradation or variety of a color; tint. 色

13.2.4 译文赏析

1. 绿艳闲且静，红衣浅复深。

译文：Her green leaves stay free and serene;

Her red blouse does glisten and sheen.

赏析："绿"和"艳"两个词是指的碧绿鲜艳的叶子。对比强烈，色泽鲜艳。本句中，译者使用了增词的手段，增加了物主代词 her，将红牡丹拟人化。同时 serene 和 sheen 形成尾韵。译文两行都有七个词，无论在字数上还是结构上，对仗非常工整，不仅做到了形似，还做到了意思的对等。

2. 花心愁欲断，春色岂知心。

译文：The sadness cuts her through, so smart;

Do the hues of spring know her heart?

赏析：愁欲断，形容伤心到极点。本句的主题为牡丹，译者将原文的拟人修辞翻译出来，使原文的形象跃然纸上。为了形成一对尾韵，译者将 smart 和 heart 放置最后，读起来朗朗上口。"花心"指的是牡丹所想，所以译者翻译为 sadness cuts…through，非常巧妙。同时，译者将肯定句处理为疑问句，更能翻译出原句的悲伤意境，也就是我们只知道花的鲜艳，却不知花的忧愁，对于自然风景认识摹写深处于"心"。最后一句 Do the hues of spring know her heart? 读起来给人以无尽的遐想，同时也完美再现了王维诗歌的意境美。

13.3　黄　雀　痴

13.3.1　诗歌背景

封建社会的伦理关系和道德观念在王维的咏物诗中也有所揭示，诗中描写了黄雀辛苦哺育："一一口衔食"，但当黄雀把幼儿"养得成毛衣""到大喍啾解游飏"时，幼儿却都"各自东西南北飞"，老黄雀只落得个"独自归"，孤凄落寞。诗人所描绘的黄雀的艺术形象，暗喻着封建社会的家庭关系，饱含着自己的哀怨和感慨。自古以来，不只是黄雀，天下所有的父母对待自己的孩子都是这样。

13.3.2　古诗原文

黄　雀　痴

黄雀痴，

黄雀痴，

谓言青縠是我儿。

一一口衔食，

养得成毛衣。

到大喍啾解游飏，

各自东西南北飞。

薄暮空巢上，

羁雌独自归。

凤凰九雏亦如此，

慎莫愁思憔悴损容辉。

13.3.3 古诗译文

The Loving Siskin

The loving siskin,

The loving siskin,

It says the chicks are my sons together,

I feed them morsel by morsel,

Now they are all growing feather.

When they chirp, chirp and spread their wings to ply,

East, west, north, south they will by themselves fly.

Now dusk falls on the nest so soon;

A stay bird comes back all alone.

A phoenix has nine sons, all like this,

Do not worry, do not pine, do not go amiss.

（赵彦春 译）

◎ 注释

1. siskin：any of several small, cardueline finches, especially Carduelis spinus, of Europe. 黄雀

2. morsel：a bite, mouthful, or small portion of food, candy, etc. 一一口

3. chirp：to make a characteristic short, sharp sound, as small birds and certain insects. 啁啾

4. ply：to run or travel regularly over a fixed course or between certain places, as a boat, bus, etc. 游飏

5. phoenix：an auspicious bird in Chinese mythology, the king of all birds, which only perches on parasol trees and eats bamboo shoots. 凤凰

6. pine：to yearn deeply；suffer with longing；long painfully（often followed by *for*）. 思憔悴

7. amiss：in a mistaken way. 损容辉

13.3.4　译文赏析

1. *黄雀痴，黄雀痴，谓言青鷇是我儿*。

译文：The loving siskin，The loving siskin，

　　　　It says the chicks are my sons together.

赏析："青鷇"的"鷇"，也就是"鸟"，该词的意思是青色的雀雏，译者译为 chicks，使用了增词的译法，增加 together，与下文中的 feather 形成尾韵。译者还使用了重复的修辞，重复"The loving siskin"一词，达到了强调本首诗的主题、加深印象和加强韵律的效果。重复是本句的艺术特征，起到了加强语气、深化印象的作用，达到了语用效果。

2. *一一口衔食，养得成毛衣*。

译文：I feed them morsel by morsel，

　　　　Now they are all growing feather.

赏析：为了译文的流畅性，译者继续将本句的视角调整为 I，译为 I feed them...同时，together 和 feather 形成一对尾韵，也就是重复 /ðə/ 的音，产生了优美悦耳的效果，译者多次使用音韵修辞。"一一口"译为 mosel by morsel，采用直译的方式，衬托出了作者所看到的景象，不仅还原了原文意境，而且简洁明了，很有画面感。

3. *到大啁啾解游飏，各自东西南北飞*。

译文：When they chirp，chirp and spread their wings to ply.

　　　　East，west，north，south they will by themselves fly.

赏析：着墨于物的声、色，是王维咏物诗的特色。"啁啾"形容鸟叫声，写得神韵飞扬、生动自然。译者使用了重复的手法，chirp 重复了两次，营造了一种画面感。同时，"游飏"是飞翔的意思，即轻盈地飘动，译者使用增词，将其翻译为 spread their wings to ply，译者用 ply 一词，表往来之意。而且 ply 和 fly 两词同为"飞翔"之意，不仅保证了词语的丰富性，而且押尾韵，有一种韵律美。同时，east 和 west、north 和 south 分别形成一对尾韵，句内有 by 和 fly 也押了 /aɪ/ 这个音的尾韵，达到了音-形-意的统一。

4. **薄暮空巢上，羁雌独自归**。

译文：Now dusk falls on the nest so soon；

A stay bird comes back all alone.

赏析：为了保证字数的对等，本句译者使用了增词的译法，在最后增加 soon，所以 soon 和 alone 形成了一对尾韵。在句子中，"羁雌"的意思是失偶的雌鸟，吕延济注："羁雌，孤鸟也。"译者译为 stay bird。

5. **凤凰九雏亦如此，慎莫愁思憔悴损容辉**。

译文：A phoenix has nine sons，all like this，

Do not worry，do not pine，do not go amiss.

赏析：韵律是诗歌中重要的要素，为了体现诗歌的节奏感，常常用韵脚押韵，而诗歌最难的是翻译其固定的韵律模式，由于语音的差异，译者并没有遵循原文的韵脚，而是在这一句中寻找到押韵的新韵脚。作者在字数上保证了一致性，不仅对仗工整，而且 this 和 amiss 形成尾韵，非常巧妙。

第十四章 咏物赞歌

14.1 新秦郡松树歌

14.1.1 诗歌背景

王维的咏物诗歌，"因物兴怀""借物抒情"，所描摹的物象是多种多样的，所抒发的感情是深沉殷实的。他抓住物体习性的某一特点加以表现，从而融合自己的情怀，揭示生活的某一侧面。诗中，"为君颜色高且闲，亭亭迥出浮云间"抓住了青松的本质特征，显示了青松耸立山上、傲然特出、高入云间的神态。而"不见君，心相忆，此心向君君应识"，则是直抒自己对松树的思念和向往，从而表现出诗人高洁不凡、傲然不屈的品格，使"物"和"情"自然地融为一体。该诗主要歌颂了松树的坚贞品性，表达了作者对松树的赞美。

14.1.2 古诗原文

新秦郡松树歌

青青山上松，

数里不见今更逢。

不见君，心相忆，

此心向君君应识。

为君颜色高且闲，

亭亭迥出浮云间。

14.1.3 古诗译文

A Song of Pines in New Ch'in

The green pines on the mountains there,

No more for a mile, loom to me once more.

You out of my sight,

You inside my heart,

Don't you know your heart, your love I long for.

High above in solitude you are free;

Amid clouds floating high you seem to be.

（赵彦春 译）

◎ 注释

1. New Ch'in：a prefecture founded in the first year of Heaven Bliss (742 A. D. -756 A. D.), changed to Unicorn Town the first year of Gen Begun (758 A. D. -760 A. D.). 新秦

2. loom：to weave (something) on a loom. 逢

3. pine：any evergreen, coniferous tree of the genus Pinus, having long, needle-shaped leaves, certain species of which yield timber, turpentine, tar, pitch, etc. 松

4. in solitude：the state of being alone, especially when you find this pleasant. 颜色

14.1.4 译文赏析

1. 青青山上松，数里不见今更逢。

译文：The green pines on the mountains there,

No more for a mile, loom to me once more.

赏析：诗人将松树拟人化，刻画了松树雄劲秀丽的形貌，又表现了其孤高安闲的气质，"数里不见今更逢"，我们从这一句可以理解到松树离作者数里远，译者将其译为 no more for a mile。同时，"今更逢"的翻译，译者采取了更加偏向结果的译法，once more 的使用具有前瞻性。

2. **不见君，心相忆，此心向君君应识。**

译文：You out of my sight, You inside my heart,

Don't you know your heart, your love I long for.

赏析：本句中连用了三个"君"字，频频呼唤，直抒对松树的思念和向往，所以在译文中，也体现了译者的受众意识，将"君"一词全部译为 you，拉近了与读者的距离。同时，"此心向君君应识"，译者坚持了意义的对等，将陈述句转化为疑问句，更好地翻译出了原句中作者对于松树的向往。

3. **为君颜色高且闲，亭亭迥出浮云间。**

译文：High above in solitude you are free；

Amid clouds floating high you seem to be.

赏析："颜色"指的是气质仪度，译者在这里翻译为 in solitude，体现了松树的气质和仪度，并没有专注于字对字的对等，而是将词语意义翻译出来。"闲"指的是闲逸，译为 free；"高"一词，译为 high above，进行前置，强调了松树的气度高。另外，"迥出"是高出的意思，为了保证 free 和 be 押韵，将"迥出浮云间"进行了位置的调整，you are free 和 you seem to be 对仗非常工整，达到了形式上的对等。

14.2　赋得清如玉壶冰

14.2.1　诗歌背景

"玉壶冰"最早的出处是鲍照的《代白头吟》，代表气节风骨。十九岁的王维参加京兆府试，便以"清如玉壶冰"为题写下了这首名篇。《赋得清如玉壶冰》这首诗中，诗人让多种事物与玉壶冰互相映照，突出了玉壶冰的美质。"素冰""清心"中，诗人抓住了色彩的特点，表现了物的姿色，恰到好处地表达了感情。诗人不拘泥于单纯的物体描述，还拿自己与玉壶冰相比，在结尾还直抒胸臆，表达了自己追求高洁不凡的极致。"若向夫君比，清心尚不如"，本句直截了当、自然亲切，唤起读者的共鸣。

14.2.2 古诗原文

赋得清如玉壶冰

玉壶何用好，

偏许素冰居。

未共销丹日，

还同照绮疏。

抱明中不隐，

含净外疑虚。

气似庭霜积，

光言砌月馀。

晓凌飞鹊镜，

宵映聚萤书。

若向夫君比，

清心尚不如。

14.2.3 古诗译文

As Clear as Ice in the Jade Pot

What's the best use of a jade pot?

It's best for ice, for others not.

It does not thaw beneath the sun,

As if the window's brightly shone.

It's transparent and clear throughout;

There is nothing in, one may doubt.

It's pure as if there gathers frost,

As can outshine the steps so glossed.

At morn, it's like a mirror bright;

> At night, it offers fireworm light.
>
> If we compare you with the ice,
>
> You are far better, clear and nice.

（赵彦春 译）

◎ 注释

1. jade pot：a pot usually alluding to the integrity or purity of the holder's heart. 玉壶

2. thaw：to pass or change from a frozen to a liquid or semiliquid state；melt. 销

3. transparent：allowing you to see through it. 不隐

4. outshine：to be more impressive than somebody/something；to be better than somebody/something. 徐

5. fireworm：the larva of any of several moths，as Rhopobota naevana（black-headed fireworm），which feeds on the leaves of cranberries and causes them to wither. 萤

14.2.4 译文赏析

1. 玉壶何用好，偏许素冰居。

译文：What's the best use of a jade pot?

It's best for ice, for others not.

赏析：本句以设问形式，使诗意更显生动。"何用"意为"为什么"。"素冰"为洁白的冰，译者将"素冰"作为一个语言单位，将其处理为 ice。在句子的处理方式上，译者很灵活地处理了"偏许素冰居"，译者并未追求字对字的形式上的对等，而是注重意思上的对应。而且将一个句子拆分成两个小句，使读者更能接受意思。

2. 未共销丹日，还同照绮疏。

译文：It does not thaw beneath the sun,

As if the window's brightly shone.

赏析："销丹日"指冰在赤日下融化，译者译为 thaw 而不是 melt，因为 melt 泛指任何事物从固体变成液体的过程，而 thaw 单单指开始解冻，但是未变成液体，也用来体现素冰免于被赤日所融的命运，反衬出玉壶之功用。下一句中，"绮疏"指的是窗户上雕刻的花纹，也指刻有花纹的窗户。译者采用了省略译法，译为 window，并且将主动意识转化为

被动意识，即 is brightly shone。译者添加 brightly 一词，更加点出前句中素冰之"明"。本句在字数上做到了工整对仗，而且 sun 和 shone 押尾韵。

3. 抱明中不隐，含净外疑虚。

译文：It's transparent and clear throughout;

There is nothing in, one may doubt.

赏析：在前一句中，"不隐"翻译为 transparent and clear，来表达玉壶的透明；后一句中，译者注重读者的感受，为了和前一句的透明形成对应，先翻译了"虚"这个词，译者准确地选择了句子的焦点。最后 throughout 和 doubt 押尾韵，非常巧妙。

4. 气似庭霜积，光言砌月馀。

译文：It's pure as if there gathers frost,

As can outshine the steps so glossed.

赏析：本句的"气"和上一句的"虚"相互呼应，译者在翻译的时候采用了意译的翻译方式，增加了 pure 一词，描摹玉壶中围绕着素冰的冰雾，此亦衬写素冰。下一句，"言"是"料，知"的意思；砌为台阶的边沿，写素冰之光与台阶边沿之光相比更胜之有余，所以用了 outshine 一词，形容素冰之光亮。

5. 晓凌飞鹊镜，宵映聚萤书。

译文：At morn, it's like a mirror bright;

At night, it offers fireworm light.

赏析：本句紧接着上句的光来写，衬写素冰之亮。本句对仗非常工整，在字数上、形式上、典故上都做到了统一。比如"晓"是早上，译者译为 at morn，"宵"是晚上，译者译为 at night。从早、晚两个对比的时间段来写，可见素冰之光亮昼夜不变。"飞鹊镜"是古镜的一种，传说可以照见妻子之心，译者采用了意译的翻译方式，将意义翻译出来：mirror bright；同时，"聚萤书"典故指的是车胤聚萤用以照书。不仅如此，在音韵上，bright 和 light 也押了尾韵。

6. 若向夫君比，清心尚不如。

译文：If we compare you with the ice,

You are far better, clear and nice.

赏析：本句中，"夫君"以称友朋，此指玉壶冰。"玉壶冰"胜于妻、友，真如知己。

译者将自我提及语添加，如 we，更能拉近与听众的距离，而且意思也表达得更明白。"清心尚不如"中，使用拟人的手法，显示作者对素冰清高坚贞气节的倾慕，意味深远。本句的翻译，作者并未将"清心"一词译出，而是将修辞翻译，达到了形神兼备的效果。同时，ice 和 nice 押了尾韵，非常有韵律。

14.3　青　雀　歌

14.3.1　诗歌背景

这是王维的一首咏物诗。咏物诗歌物言志，以此表达自己的政治理想，展示文人博大而洒脱的情怀。"青雀"这一物象是一种平凡的鸟，王维以青雀自比，虽因自己"翅羽短"而不能食玉山禾，犹如不能得高官厚禄，不能得道成仙，但总比那些为"争上下"而唧唧于空仓的黄雀好。这表明他不肯为争空名虚誉而混同常人，也表明他视官场如"空仓"的超脱形象。诗歌采取先抑后扬的写法，借青雀写出诗人的高洁傲岸之情。

14.3.2　古诗原文

青 雀 歌

青雀翅羽短，

未能远食玉山禾。

犹胜黄雀争上下，

唧唧空仓复若何。

14.3.3　古诗译文

A Song of the Blue Sparrow

The blue sparrow spreads its wings short

And can't eat grain from the mountains afar.

It challenges yellow sparrows in their sport;

Chirp, chirp, to the void barn crying they are.

（赵彦春 译）

◎ 注释

1. blue sparrow: a bird looking like a sparrow or a little turtledove. A verse in *The Book of Songs* reads like this: The little turtledove cries / And darts towards the skies. 青雀

2. chirp: to make a characteristic short, sharp sound, as small birds and certain insects. 唧唧

3. void barn: an empty space. 空仓

14.3.4　译文赏析

1. 青雀翅羽短，未能远食玉山禾。

译文: The blue sparrow spreads its wings short.

And can't eat grain from the mountains afar.

赏析: "青雀"是一种鸟名，头部黑色，腹背皆淡灰褐色，译者一如既往将青色译为 blue，即 blue sparrow。玉山禾是传说中的昆仑山的木禾，所以译者用了 afar 这个词。前一句的 short 和后一句的 afar 形成强烈的对比，表达了青雀作为一种小型鸟类，翅膀短小，飞不到遥远的仙山。

2. 犹胜黄雀争上下，唧唧空仓复若何。

译文: It challenges yellow sparrows in their sport;

Chirp, chirp, to the void barn crying they are.

赏析: "黄雀"为鸟名。雄鸟上体浅黄绿色，腹部白色而腰部稍黄。属于常见鸟类，所以译为 yellow sparrow，"唧唧"比喻鸟声，所以处理为 chirp。"空仓"译者理解为 void barn，讲充满世俗之气的黄雀唧唧对空仓乱叫，但是青雀不理会世俗的黄雀唧唧之声。诗歌采取先抑后扬的写法，借青雀写出诗人的高洁傲岸之情。

第十五章 禅意幽幽

15.1 文杏馆

15.1.1 诗歌背景

"文杏馆"是诗人隐居的辋川别业附近的一个风景点。前二句写对建馆所用材料之选择，形容文杏馆建筑材料的珍奇与不同凡俗。"文杏"，杏树之一种，极名贵。后二句让人联想到文杏馆的周边环境之幽雅与布局位置之高。全诗的艺术构思都是象征化的。文杏、香茅均为名贵珍稀之物，用作建筑材料，是一个超凡脱俗的理想境界，诗中洋溢着释情佛意，却没有一句释言佛语，这是象征的妙用。

15.1.2 古诗原文

文杏馆

文杏裁为梁，
香茅结为宇。
不知栋里云，
去作人间雨。

15.1.3 古诗译文

Ginko Pavilion

Of ginko wood the beam is made;

With balmy thatch the roof is laid.

The clouds inside it, you don't know

Make a rain to the world below.

（赵彦春 译）

◎ **注释**

1. Ginko Pavilion：one of the several pavilions with railings on the southeast mountainside of Mt. Wangch'uan. 文杏

2. beam：a long, thick piece of wood, metal, or concrete, especially used to support weight in a building or other structure. 梁

3. balmy thatch：a kind of thatch that gives off a smell of balm, growing mainly in the Hsiang River, the Long River and the Huai river areas. 香茅

4. roof：the covering that forms the top of a building. 宇

15.1.4 译文赏析

1. 文杏裁为梁，香茅结为宇。

译文：Of ginko wood the beam is made；

With balmy thatch the roof is laid.

赏析："文杏"也就是银杏。俗称白果树。古代贵族人家经常用银杏木料作房梁，译者译为 ginko wood。"香茅结为宇"，意谓用香茅结屋檐。香茅是一种有香味的茅草，所以译者以字为翻译单位，将"香"和"茅"都译出，即 balmy thatch，诗歌前两句以"文杏""香茅"结馆，是暗写房屋主人心中的忠贞之德。译者翻译这两联的时候，将主动转为被动，更加地客观和接近结果。另外，made 和 laid 形成一对尾韵。

2. 不知栋里云，去作人间雨。

译文：The clouds inside it, you don't know.

Make a rain to the world below.

赏析：译者将"栋里云"作为翻译单位，翻译为 clouds inside it。"栋里云"也写出文杏馆地势之高，缥缈云间。原诗全诗都无主语，但却至诚至性，有天人合一的境界。"人间雨"译为 a rain to the world，同样是采取了以词语为翻译单位，并且"人间雨"是从"栋里

云"中来，赋予了文杏馆人情味。而且译者增加了 below，与前一句中的高形成对比，显示出远离尘世又关心尘世，很巧妙地关合了诗人隐居的心态。译者在翻译时，增加了 you，凸显了人的独立精神。

15.2　左掖梨花

15.2.1　诗歌背景

一千三百多年前暮春的一天，唐朝皇宫大明宫麟德殿左侧（即左掖）的门下省庭院中的梨花盛开，花片如雪，香气浓郁。王维、皇甫冉、丘为三位诗人办完公务，便以《左掖梨花》为题，即兴吟诗。其他两位诗人的创作如下：冷艳全欺雪，馀香乍入衣。春风且莫定，吹向玉阶飞（丘为）。巧解迎人笑，偏能乱蝶飞。春风时入户，几片落朝衣（皇甫冉）。

15.2.2　古诗原文

左掖梨花

闲洒阶边草，
轻随箔外风。
黄莺弄不足，
衔入未央宫。

15.2.3　古诗译文

Pear Blossoms at Undergate Department

How the grass by the steps admire!

With wind from out the screen they fly.

The orioles send them to Non-end,

As they cannot keep them all by.

（赵彦春 译）

◎ **注释**

1. blossom：a flower or a mass of flowers，especially on a fruit tree. 花

2. Undergate Department：the most powerful administrative organization of the Tang Empire. 左掖

3. oriole：a bright yellow bird with black wings. 黄莺

4. Non-end：Non-end Palace built in the Han Dynasty，referring to a Tang palace in this poem. 未央宫

15.2.4 译文赏析

1. **闲洒阶边草，轻随幕外风。**

译文：How the grass by the steps admire!

With wind from out the screen they fly.

赏析：在译文中，译者用 how 一词加强语气，凸显出诗人对阶边草或者大自然的喜爱。下一句中的"箔"字，在古汉语中"箔"意为"帘子"，译者译为 screen，为熟词生义。而 wind 指轻风，从 they fly 可看出，译者在夸大描述。一句 How the grass by the steps admire 的重读音节在前半句，非重读音节在后句，所以第一句是扬抑格（Trochee）。第二句 With wind from out the screen they fly 的重读音节在后半句，非重读音节在前半句，总的来说第二句应该是抑扬格（Iambus），两句都由八音节（四步）构成。the grass 对等 wind，by 对等 out，the steps 对等 the screen，admire 对等 they fly，所以译者保证了结构、形式的对等。

2. **黄莺弄不足，衔入未央宫。**

译文：The orioles send them to Non-end，

As they cannot keep them all by.

赏析："未央"在古汉语中的意思是"永远快乐，没有穷尽"。译者将其译为 Non（未）和 end（央），即 Non-end（未央宫），所以是新创词（coined word）。第三句 The orioles send them to Non-end 为抑扬格（Iambus），前半句为非重读音节，后半句为重读音节。第

四句 As they cannot keep them all by 同理也为抑扬格（Iambus）。在音韵方面，第三句有九个音节，第四句有八个音节，鉴于不少于两个音节且不多于三个音节为一步，所以第三四句同样是四步。整首译诗以抑扬格为主，所以判断该译诗为四步抑扬格（Iambic Tetrameter）。在结构和形式上，本首译诗形式上对仗，The orioles 对等 they，send 对等 cannot keep，Non-end 对等 them。第三句 The orioles send them to Non-end 翻译的是"黄莺"和"衔入未央宫"。第四句 As they cannot keep them all by 翻译的是"弄不足"。另外，为了保持句子的连贯性和逻辑性，增添 as 衔接第三句，此为增译法（adding method）。

15.3 酬黎居士淅川作

15.3.1 诗歌背景

"莲花"是佛教中的重要用语，象征着庄严净土。在这首诗歌中，王维实现了对"莲花"意象的创构，表现了诗人清净无染的心境。古诗名句"著处是莲花，无心变杨柳"中，"莲花"指净土，"无心"指不起妄心，指达到了无妄心的境界。"气味当共知，那能不携手"也是出自这首诗，气味指的是药和茶，代指两人志趣相同，展现自己修禅的决心和心得。

15.3.2 古诗原文

酬黎居士淅川作

侬家真个去，

公定随侬否。

著处是莲花，

无心变杨柳。

松龛藏药裹，

石唇安茶臼。

气味当共知，

那能不携手。

15.3.3 古诗译文

Thanking Li, a Lay Buddhist in Rustle River

I will go out of the world now;

Are you sure you will follow me?

Lo, lotus blossoms here and there,

In Nature, like nature we'll be.

Tea mortar placed beside the rock;

Herbal bag stored in the pine shrine.

The taste, the flavor we both know;

Why don't we join hands to combine?

（赵彦春 译）

◎ **注释**

1. Rustle River: Rustle River County, Hsichuan if transliterated, in Southshine, Honan Province. 淅川

2. tea mortar: a receptacle of hard material, having a bowl-shaped cavity in which substances are reduced to powder with a pestle. 茶臼

3. pine shrine: a building or other shelter, often of a stately or sumptuous character, enclosing the remains or relics of a saint or other holy person and forming an object of religious veneration and pilgrimage. 松龛

15.3.4 译文赏析

1. 侬家真个去，公定随侬否。

译文：I will go out of the world now;

Are you sure you will follow me?

赏析："侬家"指的是作者自己，通过下一句所说的莲花，我们可以猜测作者一心追求幽静隐居的禅宗生活，所以译者将"真个去"，就是"真的要走了"，译为 go out of the world，更能表达作者追求幽静隐居的生活。"否"是语末助词，表示询问。这两句使用的翻译方式为直译法，简单明了，意思通达。

2. 著处是莲花，无心变杨柳。

译文：Lo, lotus blossoms here and there,

In Nature, like nature we'll be.

赏析：本句是整首诗出名的句子，"著处"是显著之处的意思，译者译为 here and there；后一句，译者并未采用直译的方法，并没有真的将"杨柳"译出，而是采取意译的方法，表达出不会在官场逢迎应酬的意思，所以译为 like nature we'll be，达到了意义的对等，达到了言无尽、意无穷的效果。并且 be 和 me 形成一对尾韵。

3. 松龛藏药裹，石唇安茶臼。

译文：Tea mortar placed beside the rock;

Herbal bag stored in the pine shrine.

赏析："石唇"译为 rock，"茶臼"译为 tea mortar，采用了被动语态作后置定语；后一句中，"龛"为供奉神佛或神主的石室，译者将"松龛"作为翻译单位，处理为 pine shrine，译者调整了翻译的顺序，先翻译后一句，再翻译前一句，保证了 shrine 和后一句中 combine 的押韵。

4. 气味当共知，那能不携手。

译文：The taste, the flavor we both know;

Why don't we join hands to combine?

赏析：本句指的是"药"和"茶"气味相同，代指两人的志趣相同。"气味"一词，可以将其看成一个翻译单位，译为 taste 和 flavor，但是译者使用了重复的方式，用同位语来连接。"那能不携手"采用反问的语气，其实更加强调了自己修禅的决心和心得。译者增添了 combine 一词，使得译文更加偏向结果，也使读者更加明白携手的目的。就主题意义和功能而言，借助 we 这一重复修辞深化了"物我合一"的概念。

第六部分 送别诗

第十六章　悲 伤 惜 别

16.1　送元二使安西

16.1.1　诗歌背景

　　《送元二使安西》是一首非常著名的送别诗，是友朋惜别的千古绝唱。"送"字既直接点明本诗的主题——送别，又表明作者从长安送到渭城的程程相送、依依不舍，与挥手而"别"的潇洒形成对比。全诗共四句，描绘了清晨雨后诗人在客舍设宴，为西出阳关的朋友饯行的场景与情愫。前两句写景，构建了送别的画面，巧妙地使用了"尘"与"柳"这类中国文化意象暗喻离别，而后两句则以劝酒为切入点，抒发了诗人真挚又耐人寻味的离别之情。"柳""留"谐音更显景中情语，为中国文化熏陶下的读者所不难提取。前两句展现了细雨润城、万物更新的场景。第四句中，"阳关"作为空间背景突出"故人"，"阳关"之荒凉也是一种背景反衬，以上的意象使读者最终形成一幅劝酒惜别图，读者也获得了不尽的惜别意境。

16.1.2　古诗原文

送元二使安西

渭城朝雨浥轻尘，

客舍青青柳色新。

劝君更尽一杯酒，

西出阳关无故人。

16.1.3 古诗译文

Seeing Off My Friend Yuan Second to
Pacified West as an Envoy

Dust in the town wetted by a morning rain,

The inn looks blue mid new weeping willows.

Have one more cup of wine I do maintain;

West of Sun Pass you have no old fellows.

(赵彦春 译)

◎ **注释**

1. Yuan Second：original name is Yuan Chang, ranking second at home, friend of Wang Wei. 元二

2. Pacified West：a military and political institution set up in the town of Link River in Turpan in 640 A. D. to pacifiy and govern the west regions of China. 安西

3. wet：dampen or make something moist with proper amount of wetness. 浥

4. Sun Pass：name of an old pass in today's Tunhuang, Kansu Province, an important gateway to the western regions like Jade Gate Pass. 阳关

16.1.4 译文赏析

1. 渭城朝雨浥轻尘，客舍青青柳色新。

译文：Dust in the town wetted by a morning rain,

The inn looks blue mid new weeping willows.

赏析："渭城"处理为含糊表达，译为 town，使用了节略法，体现了译者的读者意识和受众意识。同时使用被动句，以避免头重脚轻的情况。"朝雨"的译文 morning rain 采用的是具体化的翻译方式，让人有视觉的联想，更加形象和生动。第二句中，"客舍"具体化

为 inn，采用意译的方式，将"青青"翻译为 blue，根据语境的意象进行选择，这不是误译，而是用 blue 来暗示友人离别时的悲伤情景，也是诗歌翻译的叛逆现象。"柳"具体化为 weeping willows，让读者更能产生画面感。

2. **劝君更尽一杯酒，西出阳关无故人。**

译文： Have one more cup of wine I do maintain；

West of Sun Pass you have no old fellows.

赏析： 三、四句中的 I 和 you 形成人称照应，使得整个译文成为语义连贯的整体。同时，本句诗译者翻译时保证了字数的对等，"劝君更尽一杯酒"使用了前瞻的压缩，"一杯酒"翻译为 one more cup，而不仅仅是 one cup of wine，更为准确，体现了英语偏向于结果的特点，更具有前瞻性，准确地传递出"更尽"的语义与情谊。"西出阳关无故人"中将地点词语 West of Sun Pass 提前直接指向读者的心灵世界，营造了一种悲伤的境界，不仅达意，而且传神，承载了丰富的感情寄托与文体意义。故人，译者翻译为 old fellows，使用了替换法，未将具体人指出。就译诗的形式看，韵尾分别是 abab（rain，willows，maintain，fellows），再现了原诗的风貌。

16.2 临高台送黎拾遗

16.2.1 诗歌背景

诗中以杳旷广漠之川原为送别的背景，饶有蕴藉，而送别的活动在此背景中开展，亦意味深长。飞鸟归巢，强烈反衬故人之别去，这种生活场景最易引发人们的深切感受，而生成珍情重谊的爱心。全诗描写了诗人送别友人后登高远望所见景色，表达了诗人对黎拾遗离去的依依不舍之情。全诗情景交融，后二句以倦鸟飞还反衬行人远去，不言惜别而神情自见。临高台，指临近一处地势比较高的区域，道明送别的地点。黎拾遗，即王维好友黎昕，两人素有交情。"拾遗"，官名。

16.2.2 古诗原文

临高台送黎拾遗

相送临高台，

川原杳何极。

日暮飞鸟还，

行人去不息。

16.2.3 古诗译文

Ascending the Height to See Off Counselor Li

I see you off, standing on this height;

The vast plain rolls far out of sight.

Coming back, all the warblers fly;

Going back, all the travelers hie.

（赵彦春 译）

◎ 注释

1. ascending：to rise；to go up；to climb up. 临

2. counselor：an official to offer advice and recommend talents in the Tang Dynasty. It was conferred by the emperor and the chancellor. 拾遗

3. height：a particular distance above the ground. 高台

4. warbler：a small bird. 飞鸟

5. hie：to go quickly. 不息

16.2.4 译文赏析

1. 相送临高台，川原杳何极。

译文：I see you off, standing on this height;

The vast plain rolls far out of sight.

赏析：原诗的韵律是 abcb，译文的韵律为 aabb。"高台"翻译为 this height，所谓站得高，看得远，正是这般，诗人才能够极目驰骋，从而写下眼前景物、心中情思。"相送临高台"，译文使用第一人称 I 进行视角的转换，并且添加代词 this，好像读者和译者有共识，都知道这个高台，体现了译者的修辞意识，以此拉近与受众的距离。另外，"杳何极"实际指"川原"，指道路的遥远，译者译为 vast plain。除了在意思上保证忠实于原文以外，译文还选择在句组内押尾韵，如 height 和 sight。

2. 日暮飞鸟还，行人去不息。

译文：Coming back, all the warblers fly；

Going back, all the travelers hie.

赏析："还"与"去"两个词在译文中形成对比，分别将动词提前，作为伴随状语，译为 coming back 和 going back，对仗非常工整，将反义对比修辞译出，译出了诗人的百般无奈和万分不舍。译文尾韵，如 fly 和 hie 也非常押韵，调整了原文的韵律，使读者可接受，译出了诗人想要打造的氛围和意境。

16.3 送 别

16.3.1 诗歌背景

这首诗是王维送友人归隐所作，诗歌以问答的形式来说明友人归隐的原因，诗人对友人的"不得意"给予安慰，这种安慰中有对友人的同情，也有自己对现实的不满，更有自己对归隐山林的向往。诗人对友人关切爱护，既劝慰友人又对友人的归隐生活流露出羡慕之情，说明诗人对自己的现实也不很满意。诗歌语言看似简单平淡，实则词浅情深，蕴涵意味深厚。最后一句，"但去莫复问，白云无尽时。"此时此刻，作者有很多话想与朋友讲，但知道自己的朋友去意已决，王维以相当坚定的口吻表明了自己对友人归隐南山的赞许。

16.3.2 古诗原文

送 别

下马饮君酒，

问君何所之？

君言不得意，

归卧南山陲。

但去莫复问，

白云无尽时。

16.3.3 古诗译文

Good-bye

Dismounting to drink you good-bye;

"Where are you going?" I inquire.

Your aim has been unreached you sigh;

To bide the south hills you desire.

Go ahead, I will ask no more;

The white clouds there endlessly soar.

（赵彦春 译）

◎ 注释

1. dismounting：to get off a horse. 下马

2. bide：to stay or live in a place. 卧

3. south hills：Qinling mountains, now Xi'an, Shaanxi Province. 南山

4. endlessly soar：to rise quickly and smoothly up into the air. 无尽

16.3.4 译文赏析

1. **下马饮君酒，问君何所之？**

译文：Dismounting to drink you good-bye;

"Where are you going?" I inquire.

赏析：在诗歌翻译的过程中，译者注重了翻译的意美和形美。译文模仿了原诗问答体的形式，符合读者的期待，再现了原文意境。中文是散焦语言，而在译文中，译者将"下

马饮君酒"中的焦点处理为 good-bye。在音美方面，译文前四句的韵律是 abab，good-bye 和 sigh 押尾韵，形成一种音乐美；inquire 和 desire 也押尾韵，体现了译者的审美意识。

2. 君言不得意，归卧南山陲。

译文：Your aim has been unreached you sigh；
　　　　To bide the south hills you desire.

赏析："君言不得意"中，"君言"使用了省译法，you sigh 是增译，读者更能体会到作者的无奈之情，"不得意"翻译为 your aim has been unreached，处理为一个翻译单位，处理得非常灵活，形神兼备。"南山陲"是指的南山边，"陲"是边缘，译者将其处理为一个翻译单位，译为 south hills。bide 一词的处理也体现了王维的朋友去山中归隐的意象，符合读者的期待。

3. 但去莫复问，白云无尽时。

译文：Go ahead，I will ask no more；
　　　　The white clouds there endlessly soar.

赏析："但去莫复问"中，译者将句子进行拆分，拆分为肯定句和否定句。前一句为肯定句，"但去"译为 Go ahead，后一句添加了主语 I，I will ask 与前一句中的 I inquire 进行了呼应。"白云无尽时"如若直白翻译，很难再现原诗意境，本句采用增译法，增加 soar，虽然在字数上并未形成对仗，但是形成了音乐美，more 和 soar 形成了一对尾韵，soar 一词情景交融，使读者能够体会出原诗的意境。

第十七章　满怀希冀

17.1　送友人南归

17.1.1　诗歌背景

在王维为官期间，官场发生一些变动，张九龄被罢相，王维在黑暗统治期间有了归隐思想，也实践了这一思想，他隐于终南，也创作了较多的送友人归隐的诗歌，比如这首《送友人南归》。诗人运用了借景抒情、用典的表现手法，表达了诗人对友人的依依不舍以及希望友人回家孝敬父母的思想感情。特别是"遥识老莱衣"，作者使用了用典的修辞，表达了作者希望友人回家照顾双亲的期待。

17.1.2　古诗原文

送友人南归

万里春应尽，
三江雁亦稀。
连天汉水广，
孤客郢城归。
郧国稻苗秀，
楚人菰米肥。

悬知倚门望，

遥识老莱衣。

17.1.3　古诗译文

Seeing My Friend Back South

From the vast land spring should be gone；

In Three Rivers wild geese are few.

The Han is so broad，like the sky.

Back to Yington you start to go.

The State of Yun grows crops so well；

Ch'u folks have luxuriant wild rice.

Your parents may gaze now at door；

You should serve them with all supplies.

（赵彦春　译）

◎ **注释**

1. Three Rivers：referring to the River Yuan, the River Hsiang and the River Li, which flow outside Yuehshine, in today's Hunan Province. 三江

2. the Han：the Han River, the longest branch of the Long River, having an important position in Chinese history. 汉水

3. Yington：the capital city of Ch'u. 郢城

4. the State of Yun：a small state located nearby Ch'u. 郧国

5. Ch'u：a vassal state of Chough, one of the powers in the Warring States Period, conquered and annexed by Ch'in in 223 B. C. 楚人

17.1.4　译文赏析

1. 万里春应尽，三江雁亦稀。

译文：From the vast land spring should be gone；

In Three Rivers wild geese are few.

赏析：汉语的主体意识较强，从自我出发去理解、演绎和描写事物。译者在处理译文的时候，进行了主体和客体意识的转换，将"万里春应尽"的句子处理为客观句子，转换了原文中主观臆测的部分。"三江"指流经岳阳城外的沅江、澧（lǐ）江、湘江，译为 Three Rivers，采用的是直译法。同时，from the vast land 和 in Three Rivers 对仗十分工整，读起来也朗朗上口，容易为读者所接受。

2. 连天汉水广，孤客郢城归。

译文：The Han is so broad, like the sky.

Back to Yington you start to go.

赏析：本句中，将"汉水"看为一个语言单位，译为 The Han。同时，译者焦点意识明确，将 The Han is so broad 确定为焦点，like the sky 作为此焦点，所以并不失焦。并且，在下一句中，也是将主体转化为客体，避免了对"孤客"一词的猜测，而是直接译为 you。Yington 的意思是"郢城"，春秋时楚国都城，今湖北荆州一带。

3. 郧国稻苗秀，楚人菰米肥。

译文：The State of Yun grows crops so well;

Ch'u folks have luxuriant wild rice.

赏析："秀"原意为庄稼开花，译者的翻译更加接近结果，译为 grows...so well。"郧国"指的是春秋时位于楚国附近的小国，作者使用了音译，翻译为 The State of Yun。"菰米肥"中，译者将主谓短语变成偏正短语，也就是译为"肥菰米"，英文为 luxuriant wild rice，避免了译文头重脚轻的情况。

4. 悬知倚门望，遥识老莱衣。

译文：Your parents may gaze now at door;

You should serve them with all supplies.

赏析：原文中，因为中文是散焦语言，并没有发现主题，而篇章主题的选择关系到表达的流畅性，译文中选取的主语为 you，比如，your parents 指的就是友人的父母，保持了主语的一致性，加强了流畅性。"老莱衣"是用典，译者将其用典译出，用此典告知游子应早日归家孝敬双亲，译为 serve them with all supplies。译者尽可能使译文与原文的表达效果相同，从而使译文被对中国文化知之甚少的国外读者所接受。

17.2　山　中　送　别

17.2.1　诗歌背景

王维不以升迁荣辱为转移，在趋炎附势的世态炎凉里，其人情美、人性美、人格美具有强烈的震撼人心的力量。朋友失意落魄时，王维总是表现出十分的真诚和热忱，忧其忧而忿其忿，就这种感情本身而言，就具有足以让人感动涕零的情感力量。故而，其诗有时尽管淡淡数语，却胜人虚言千百。本首诗歌寥寥二十字，情意却非常浓。"相送"的一系列动作、场景和过程全都暗场处理了，妙在留白。只一"掩"字，将诗人于朋友走后的迷茫无措的神情和寂寞无聊的心态描绘得栩栩如生。再以一"问"，妙在问于分离之时，而非久去之后。他们之间的友情该有多么的亲密，我们无论如何去想象都不为过。

17.2.2　古诗原文

山中送别

山中相送罢，
日暮掩柴扉。
春草明年绿，
王孙归不归？

17.2.3　古诗译文

Parting in the Hills

In the hills, I see off my peer;

At dusk, I close my wicket door.

When grass greens everything next year,

Will you come to me any more?

（赵彦春 译）

◎ 注释

1. parting：the act or occasion of leaving a person or place. 送别

2. peer：a person who is the same age or who has the same social status as you. 友人

3. wicket：small gate or door. 柴扉

17.2.4 译文赏析

1. 山中相送罢，日暮掩柴扉。

译文：In the hills, I see off my peer;

At dusk, I close my wicket door.

赏析：由于汉语民族和英语民族的审美观存在差异，汉语的诗歌会有模糊性，而英语由于其语法机制讲究，这一句译文进行了意义的转换，译者必须让一些模糊特征变得精确，所以，在英语中，需要把模糊美转换成精确美。原文中"山中相送罢"并未体现送别的对象，但是 see off my peer，将 peer 这一对象译出，体现了英语的精确美。同时，译者还增添了主语 I，使"日暮掩柴扉"的动作主体更加明确。

2. 春草明年绿，王孙归不归？

译文：When grass greens everything next year,

Will you come to me any more?

赏析：本句中的 green 处理成动词，是使动词，意为"使变绿"。同时，也增加使用了 everything 一词。"王孙"这里指的是贵族的子孙，也就是诗中的友人，译者翻译为 you，使读者更容易接受、更容易理解。而且译者使用了增词法，增加了 any more 一词，更能体现诗歌中的离别情感。

17.3　送綦毋潜落第还乡

17.3.1　诗歌背景

綦毋潜是江南一带很著名的诗人，应试落第不是才华方面的问题。写给綦毋潜的诗中，王维对于失意者的劝慰是很有技巧的，往往以"我们"同提，表现出亲密无间、难离难舍和体贴周到。君门既远，不是因为"你我"的才能不行，也不是因为"你我"的谋略失当，实在是因为没有碰上好机遇罢了。在对被送之人本身的价值和才能充分肯定的同时，也借机发牢骚，暗含对昏晦政治的不满。而把这种悲剧的深刻原因归咎于当时的朝庭，在这首诗的开篇处已挑明。

17.3.2　古诗原文

送綦毋潜落第还乡

圣代无隐者，
英灵尽来归。
遂令东山客，
不得顾采薇。
既至君门远，
孰云吾道非。
江淮度寒食，
京洛缝春衣。
置酒临长道，
同心与我违。
行当浮桂棹，
未几拂荆扉。
远树带行客，

孤村当落晖。

吾谋适不用，

勿谓知音稀。

17.3.3 古诗译文

Adieu to Ch'ien Ch'iwu Who's Failed Grand Test

A good age does no hermit find;

There comes to court many a mind.

A recluse like you no more hide;

Or pick ferns on the mountainside.

Unlucky, in Grand Test you fail.

Who can say you are off the trail?

You passed Midland last Cold Food Day;

This year in Capital you stay.

Now on Broad Way I drink to you,

Because we will soon say adieu.

Down south you will row with an oar.

Before long, you'll ope your chaste door.

The trees afar will follow you,

Your village tinted with eve hue.

It's nothing that you are laid by;

You still have friends, no need to sigh.

(赵彦春 译)

◎ 注释

1. Adieu: goodbye. 送

2. Ch'ien Ch'iwu: Ch'ien Ch'iwu (692 A. D. -749 A. D.), a famous Tang poet, who retired to be a recluse after Lushan An's Rebellion. 綦毋潜

3. Grand Test: referring to imperial examination for selecting talents to serve as officials. 考试

4. recluse：a person who lives alone and likes to avoid other people. 东山客

5. pick ferns on the mountainside：referring to the story of Bowone and Straightthree. As they failed to admonish King Martial of Chough, they left Chough and refused to take crops reaped under the reign of Chough. They lived on fungi on Mt. Headshine and finally starved to death. 顾采薇

6. Cold Food Day：one or two days before Pure Brightness Day（the third day of the third moon each year）, the festival in memory of Chiht'ui of Chieh（？-636 B. C. ）observed without cooking for a day. In the Spring and Autmun Period, Double Ear, a prince of Chin, escaped from the disaster in his state with his follower Chiht'ui. In great deprivation, Double Ear almost starved to death, and Chiht'ui fed him with flesh cut off his thigh. When Double Ear was crowned as Lord Civil of Chin, Chiht'ui retreated to Mt. Silk Floss with his mother when feeling neglected. To have him out, Lord Civil set the mountain on fire, but Chiht'ui did not give in and was burned with his mother, hugging a tree. 寒食

7. Capital：referring to Long Peace, the capital of Tang, with a population of about one million at that time. 京洛

8. Broad Way：also known as Chang'an Broad Way. 长道

17.3.4　译文赏析

1. 圣代无隐者，英灵尽来归。遂令东山客，不得顾采薇。

译文：A good age does no hermit find；There comes to court many a mind.

A recluse like you no more hide；Or pick ferns on the mountain side.

赏析：本节原诗的韵律为 abab，译文的韵律为 aabb，读者读起来很有节奏感。译者使用了增词的方式，增加词语 find 和 mind 形成尾韵，朗朗上口。"隐者"译为 hermit，"英灵"是英华灵秀的贤才，译为 mind。下一句"遂令东山客"中，译者并未采取直译法，而是将肯定句译为否定句：no more hide；"东山客"的意思是，东晋谢安曾隐居在会稽东山，此处泛指隐居的贤才，所以将"东山客"翻译为 recluse。同时 hide 和 side 形成一对尾韵，非常巧妙。

2. 既至君门远，孰云吾道非。江淮度寒食，京洛缝春衣。

译文：Unlucky, in Grand Test you fail. Who can say you are off the trail？

You passed Midland last Cold Food Day; This year in Capital you stay.

赏析："君门远"的意思是指难以见到皇上，译者将"君门"译为 Grand Test，将其引申意思翻译出来，就是没有通过考试。"寒食"，采用直译加释意的方式，先译为 Cold Food Day。"江淮"指的是长江，是綦毋潜回家所经过的地方，所以译者进行了意译，译为 Midland，也就是中部地方。"京洛缝春衣"中，"京洛"指的是京城洛阳，所以译为 Capital。前两句中的 fail 和 trail 形成尾韵，后两句中的 day 和 stay 形成尾韵，读起来朗朗上口。

3. 置酒临长道，同心与我违。行当浮桂棹，未几拂荆扉。

译文：Now on Broad Way I drink to you, Because we will soon say adieu.

Down south you will row with an oar. Before long, you'll ope your chaste door.

赏析："长道"也称为长安道，译者译为 Broad Way，"同心"的意思是志同道合的朋友、知己，译者对其进行转化，以 we 为视角进行翻译，"违"是分别的意思，译者译为 adieu。"行当浮桂棹"中的"行当"指的是将要的意思，"棹"指划船用的工具，译为 oar，"未几拂荆扉"中，译者将"荆扉"看作一个语言单位，译为 chaste door，"未几"和"行当"形成对照，也是将要的意思，这两句中，oar 和 door 形成一对尾韵，you 和 adieu 押尾韵，读起来有韵律感。

4. 远树带行客，孤村当落晖。吾谋适不用，勿谓知音稀。

译文：The trees afar will follow you, Your village tinted with eve hue.

It's nothing that you are laid by; You still have friends, no need to sigh.

赏析：中文为散焦语言，英文为聚焦语言，所以翻译的时候，为了保持行文的流畅性，译者还是一直保持以 you 为视角进行翻译。"孤村当落晖"中，译者并未将"孤村"拆分，而是看作一个语言单位处理，译为 village。"落晖"的处理也非常灵活，译作 eve hue，更能为读者所理解。"吾谋适不用"指的是綦毋潜偶然落榜，lay by 表示落榜的意思，译者采用了被动的翻译方式，将这一事实描述得更加客观。by 和 sigh 形成一对尾韵，同时 you 和 hue 也符合押韵的原则。

第十八章 壮 志 未 酬

18.1 别辋川别业

18.1.1 诗歌背景

　　王维之前在辋川写过隐居时期的田园生活，而辋川别业是王维在陕西蓝田县宋之问辋川山庄的基础上营建的园林别墅。"别业"也就是别墅的意思。《别辋川别业》大意是依依不舍地启动车马，心情惆怅地拿出松萝。忍着告别离开，青山绿水还是那个样子。"青山"是诗人的选择，王维在其中生活，将其诗化，他寻找的是一种人生体验，以此表达离开辋川别业时的依依惜别之情。

18.1.2 古诗原文

别辋川别业

依迟动车马，
惆怅出松萝。
忍别青山去，
其如绿水何。

18.1.3 古诗译文

Good Bye to My Cottage at Wangch'uan

I hesitate to start my cart,

Though I leave the pines with a sigh.

From the green hill we go apart;

The blue stream feels hard to say bye.

(赵彦春 译)

◎ 注释

1. cart：a vehicle with two or four wheels that is pulled by a horse and used for carrying loads. 车马

2. pine：a symbol of longevity and rectitude in Chinese culture. 松萝

3. sigh：to take and then let out a long deep breath that can be heard, to show that you are disappointed, sad, tired, etc. 惆怅

18.1.4 译文赏析

1. 依迟动车马，惆怅出松萝。

译文：I hesitate to start my cart,

Though I leave the pines with a sigh.

赏析：为了保持汉语的对称和平衡，汉语的虚词少，而且句子结构中，体现思维方式的平行结构并无主从之分，主语谓语难辨，呈现出动态散点的意象美。而译文把"动车马"处理为非谓语，来凸显"迟"一词的焦点，又通过作者的视角把"出松萝"用 though 将一系列动作词语连接，层次分明。"惆怅"翻译为 sigh，与后一句的 bye 形成一对尾韵。

2. 忍别青山去，其如绿水何。

译文：From the green hill we go apart;

The blue stream feels hard to say bye.

　　赏析："忍别青山去"为无主句，译文添加了 we 一词，与前两句视角保持一致，具有连贯性。同时，译者将"忍别"一词作为一个翻译单位，译为 go apart。在下一句中，"其如绿水何"，译者增加 hard to say bye，将原文的无可奈何之感翻译得淋漓尽致，使用了前瞻的翻译方式，把诗人的情感表现得更加清楚。"绿水"翻译为 blue stream，而没有使用 green，更加体现了悲伤的情感。

18.2　送魏郡李太守赴任

18.2.1　诗歌背景

　　诗人以我观物，十分注重审美主体的心理感受，其内在情绪在寻找对应物的过程中表现出相当积极的状态而外射、同化景物使之成为其特定心态的艺术符号。比如，送别场景自古黯然凄怨，而王维笔下则时多"英雄气象"。比如，"苍茫秦川尽，日落桃林塞。"诗人潜在的用世情绪顽执地规范着他的审美取向和意象创制，外显为具有强烈自我色彩的审美形态。魏郡指的是魏洲，属河北道，治所在今河北临漳西南邺镇一带。写诗的对象是李太守，李将军也就是李太守，这首诗表达了诗人对李太守的怀念之情以及对自己内心不得志的感慨之情。

18.2.2　古诗原文

送魏郡李太守赴任

与君伯氏别，

又欲与君离。

君行无几日，

当复隔山陂。

苍茫秦川尽，

日落桃林塞。

独树临关门，

黄河向天外。

前经洛阳陌,

宛洛故人稀。

故人离别尽,

淇上转骖騑。

企予悲送远,

惆怅睢阳路。

古木官渡平,

秋城邺宫故。

想君行县日,

其出从如云。

遥思魏公子,

复忆李将军。

18.2.3 古诗译文

Seeing Off Prefect Li to His Prefecture of Way

To your brother I said good-bye;

Now to you I will say adieu.

A few days after you depart,

You'll be barred by hills green, rills blue.

The Ch'in Plain rolls far, far away;

The peach wood basks in the eve sun.

A tree stands alone by the pass;

The River out the sky does run.

Ahead you go through Loshine fields;

On the river few friends you'll see.

When all friends have gone out of sight,

You get on you cart by the Ch'i.

On tiptoe, I watch you away;

While towards Suishine you do sigh.

In Kuantu the barracks are gone;

The palaces in Yeh waste lie.

When counties of yours you inspect,

Your retinue's like clouds behind.

Now I miss Prince of Way far back,

And General Li comes to my mind.

（赵彦春　译）

◎ 注释

1. the Ch'in Plain：the area north of Ch'inridge that rolls in today's Sha'anhsi and Kansu, which belonged to the State of Ch'in in the past. 秦川

2. the River：referring to the Yellow River, the second longest river in China, flowing through Loess Plateau, hence yellow water all the way. 5,464 kilometers long, with a drainage area of 75,2443 square kilometers, it has been regarded as the cradle of Chinese civilization. 黄河

3. Loshine：Loyang if transliterated, one of the four ancient capitals in China, along with Long Peace (Hsi'an), Gold Hill (Nanking) and Peking, and it was the second largest city in the Tang Dynasty. 洛阳

4. the Ch'i：an ancient affluent of the Yellow River. 淇

5. Suishine：a county south of the Sui River, now in Shangch'iu, Honan Province. 睢阳

6. Kuantu：an old battlefield where Ts'ao Ts'ao decisively defeated Shao Yuan's army, in today's Chungmou, Honan Province. 官渡

7. Yeh：one of the eight most famous capitals in Chinese history, in today's Linchang County, Hopei Province. 邺

8. Prince of Way：Faithridge (?-243 B.C.), the youngest son of King Glare of Way, a famous militarist and politician in the Warring States Period. He was courteous to talents, attracting 3,000 hangers-on. 魏公子

9. General Li：Broad Li in full name, Kuang Li if transliterated, a renowned general who won

many battles against the Huns in the Han Dynasty. 李将军

18.2.4 译文赏析

1. 与君伯氏别，又欲与君离。君行无几日，当复隔山陂。

译文： To your brother I said good-bye; Now to you I will say adieu.

A few days after you depart, You'll be barred by hills green, rills blue.

赏析： 译者的受众意识很强，加入一些如 you, your, I 等自我提及语和读者提及语，拉近与读者的距离。比如，"伯氏"译为 your brother。同时，将"山陂"进行增译，后置为 hills green, rills blue，渲染了一种悲伤的气氛。同时，adieu 和 blue 形成一对尾韵，节奏感强。

2. 苍茫秦川尽，日落桃林塞。独树临关门，黄河向天外。

译文： The Ch'in Plain rolls far, far away; The peach wood basks in the eve sun.

A tree stands alone by the pass; The River out the sky does run.

赏析： "苍茫秦川尽"中，译者使用了重复的翻译方式，将 far 重复两次，强调和体现了秦川的广阔。中文是散焦语言，英文是聚焦语言，所以，在英译文中，译者找到句子的主题，比如"秦川""桃林""树""黄河"，例如，"日落桃林塞"真正的主题是 peach wood，"日落"为非焦点。sun 和 run 形成尾韵，读起来比较押韵。

3. 前经洛阳陌，宛洛故人稀。故人离别尽，淇上转骖騑。

译文： Ahead you go through Loshine fields; On the river few friends you'll see.

When all friends have gone out of sight, You get on you cart by the Ch'i.

赏析： 原文是无主句，但译者加入了 you 贯穿全文，与首句形成呼应，体现了译者的受众意识。"洛阳"译为 Loshine，为音译，读起来更为流畅。"故人稀"作为主谓短语，处理为偏正短语，即 few friends。"骖騑"是古代驾车的马，所以译为 cart。

4. 企予悲送远，惆怅睢阳路。古木官渡平，秋城邺宫故。

译文： On tiptoe, I watch you away; While towards Suishine you do sigh.

In Kuantu the barracks are gone; The palaces in Yeh waste lie.

赏析： 本句中地点词语比较多，"睢阳""官渡""邺"分别翻译为 Suishine, Kuantu 以及 Yeh，使用异化的翻译方式，使外国读者更能理解。另外，sigh 和 lie 押韵，朗朗上口。"企予"是踮起脚尖的意思，所以译为 on tiptoe。原文中，"悲送远"主客不分，而译文中，将"悲送远"的对象具体化，也就是李太守，所以译为 I watch you away。

5. 想君行县日，其出从如云。遥思魏公子，复忆李将军。

译文：When counties of yours you inspect, Your retinue's like clouds behind.

Now I miss Prince of Way far back, And General Li comes to my mind.

赏析：译者将"魏公子"非常精妙地翻译为 Prince of Way，这一译法可以为读者所借鉴；behind 和 mind 形成一对尾韵，处理非常得当。"遥思魏公子，复忆李将军"缺少主语，在本句译文中，增添了人称主语 I，与首句的主题保持一致，而且具有互动性，更加能体现原文中依依惜别之情。

18.3　送刘司直赴安西

18.3.1　诗歌背景

王维生活在唐代，唐代的中国是一个先进的国家，经济繁荣，文学领域更是一片欣欣向荣的气象，诗人本人也渴望建功立业。王维在这首诗歌中，也表现了自己积极向上的思想追求。王维渴望有机会施展自己的才华与报负，渴望能有卓著政绩，对国家有所贡献。所以此诗前两联写景，介绍友人赴边的道路情况，指出路途遥远、寂寞荒凉、环境恶劣；第三联以想象描绘了丝绸之路上的特异风光，仍是写景，但色调感情陡转；最后一联希望刘司直出塞建功立业，弘扬国威，同时也寄寓着作者自己的报国豪情。

18.3.2　古诗原文

送刘司直赴安西

绝域阳关道，

胡沙与塞尘。

三春时有雁，

万里少行人。

苜蓿随天马，

蒲桃逐汉臣。

当令外国惧，

不敢觅和亲。

18.3.3　古诗译文

Seeing Off Justice Liu to Pacified West

The Sun Pass road rolls far and far,

Full of border dust and Hun sand.

Only a few wild geese in spring,

And few people on the vast land.

Clover, Pegasus and grape seed

Will be carried back to Mid-plain.

This will deter the aliens much

From imposing marriage again.

（赵彦春　译）

◎ 注释

1. Sun Pass：name of an old pass in today's Tunhuang, Kansu Province, an important gateway to the western regions like Jade Gate Pass. 阳关

2. Hun：one of barbaric nomadic Asian people who frequently invaded China, a general term referring to all northern or western invaders. 胡

3. Pegasus：a kind of horse from west of China, usually with wings in fairy tales, also known as sky-horse. In many cases it is used as a metaphor for a fine horse. 天马

4. imposing marriage：feudal dynasties used marriage relations to make peace with rulers of frontier tribes. 觅和亲

18.3.4　译文赏析

1. 绝域阳关道，胡沙与塞尘。三春时有雁，万里少行人。

译文：The Sun Pass road rolls far and far, Full of border dust and Hun sand.

Only a few wild geese in spring, And few people on the vast land.

赏析："绝域"指的是极远的地域，所以译者使用了重复的翻译方式，将 far 一词重复了两次，体现了地域之远。"胡沙"与"塞尘"理解为一个翻译单位，所以翻译为 Hun sand 和 border dust。同时，对"胡沙"与"塞尘"的翻译位置做了调整，以便 sand 和 land 押尾韵。译文中的"时有"和"少"翻译为 few，形成一种对照，比较工整。

2. 苜蓿随天马，蒲桃逐汉臣。当令外国惧，不敢觅和亲。

译文：Clover, Pegasus and grape seed, Will be carried back to Mid-plain.

This will deter the aliens much, From imposing marriage again.

赏析：译者将"苜蓿""天马""蒲桃"进行了位置的调整，Mid-plain 放在句尾，与 again 形成一对尾韵，读起来朗朗上口。在本句中，使用 will be carried back to 作为被动用法，将中文的意境美转换为精确美。"觅和亲"中的"觅"一词使用得很恰当，翻译为 impose，把强迫的意思翻译出来。